"Lekker Lees!"

Enjoy the Read!

SEE-SAW

Hank Muni

H. Muni

ISBN 978-1540704313

 This edition first published in Canada by Henk Muni.

Book design by CCS-Crystal Clear Solutions.

Henk Muni
www.henkmuni.com

SEE-SAW

EVERYONE HAS A TIPPING POINT

Henk Muni

Dedication

To Oom Piet, who said "Henkeman moenie,"
and my lifelong friend Riaan Smit.

See-saw:

Definition of see-saw from Oxford Dictionaries

noun

A long plank balanced in the middle on a fixed support, on each end of which children sit and swing up and down by pushing the ground alternately with their feet.

A situation characterized by rapid, repeated changes from one state or condition to another.

verb

[No object]

Change rapidly and repeatedly from one position, situation, or condition to another and back again.

Origin: Mid-17th century (originally used by sawyers as a rhythmical refrain): reduplication of the verb saw (symbolic of the sawing motion).

CHAPTER 1

THE JOKER'S SMILE

I saw my silhouette reflected in Michael's huge pupil as the adrenaline pushed his emerald green iris to a thin sliver.

A gust of wind slammed against the building and rushed icy snow into my face. I squinted and shielded my eyes with my hands. The wind tugged at Michael's shirt and ruffled his hair.

He let out his final words one by one.

"Why ... so ... serious?"

He fell backward, slowly, his eyes locked on mine, his calm smile denying the snow-covered tarmac thirteen stories below. As he passed the point of no return, his fingers reflexively grabbed at the air, but he quickly accepted the inevitable, opened his palms, and spread his arms backwards in an arch.

Joseph Campbell said, 'If you are falling ... dive.'

His body appeared relaxed as he reached terminal velocity. His shirt snapped and fluttered. As he struck the tarmac my heart ripped out of my chest, and my shoulders and head dropped. My vision was a watery shimmer.

My best friend was dead.

As the snow cloud cleared, I could see the crimson enlarge around his head. His green eyes had lost their focus and stared blankly into space, but a fake Joker's smile was stuck to his face. How ironic for Michael to have died with that grimace. Risus sardonicus is the medical term for the painful grimace of a man dying from tetanus, and it was the real-life template for the cartoon Joker smile—the sardonic smile.

It was unlike Michael to smile in such a way, but his true talent was faking sincerity.

He could wear a warm smile like a mask. Old ladies would blush and young nurses would break eye contact. I could see right through it, but I had learned that no one else could. I'd known him for more than twenty years, since before he could perfect it. So corny: I could sometimes imagine the little sparkle of his eye tooth.

The scene below me was surreal, like a scene pencil-sketched. The clear vertical lines of the building streaked down and converged on the fallen villain lying in the snow. I always knew Michael's death would somehow be spectacular, but this was truly over the top. He was right in front of the hospital entrance, splayed out as a huge red blotch on the white, snow-covered tarmac, with a grimace on his face. Like the last page of a classic comic book, I imagined big graphic letters in a jagged-edged comment bubble: *The Joker Dies.*

I shivered.

It didn't feel real. It wasn't real, was it?

Dr. Michael Clarke, my friend, died with the Joker's smirk on his face, "laughing to his death." He'd smirked, just for show. I realized he had purposefully changed the expression on his face in his last moment of life. Freakishly calculated; staging a final scene for eternity. So exactly like Michael.

He'd accepted the inevitable and completed the scene.

I stood there frozen with the wind tugging at my clothes and the snow hitting my face, numbing it further. Frozen. Unable to move. Petrified.

Petrified. The single word that brought me to this roof, this disaster, at this point in time. Who would have guessed we'd end up here?

The shivers started coming more regularly.

I started to tremble. My hands were shaking, and the void suddenly wanted to suck me down too. My eyes were fixed on his smile and it drew me in. All I could hear was a high-pitched ping ringing in my ears: *tinnitus.*

Ping.

It blocked every other sound, and was so loud it stung behind my eyes and created spots in my vision: *scotoma?*

Am I getting a migraine? The lonely question floated inside my head.

I could see the poor, flabbergasted security guard circle around Michael below. He appeared white as a ghost and shaken. After quickly glancing upwards, he dove onto the ground, fumbling at Michael's neck for a pulse.

Why bother?

I could see him throw his head back and yell, "Code blue!"

Ping!

Then silence.

A tsunami of sound rolled in. The air filled with white noise, alarms, and people yelling. Screams surrounded me. Chaos.

I looked at my hands. My "healing hands," as Dad called them. "Always look after your hands, Pieter. They're your future, son." They trembled now. It started with a slight tremor, but I could suppress it. The tremor encouraged a tremble. The shaking started. I was losing it. My knees buckled. I couldn't stand, I couldn't move. I needed to snap out of it. *Get a grip, man.* The void pulled on me. I just needed to let go. "Control freak, just let *go*!" were words Michael would always throw my way. As I stared at his grimace, I could hear him clearly inside my head.

Just let go.

The void drew me in. The sense of weightlessness was intoxicating. I felt I could reach out to a world where all responsibilities would be gone. Wouldn't it be fantastic to drop this load from my shoulders like a backpack?

I started to feel light. Burden free. Weightless.

I wanted to embrace the lightness.

Silence and calm blunted out everything else.

I wanted to let it all go. I leaned into the nothingness.

"I am coming, Michael."

■ ■ ■

From nowhere, a meteorite of muscle hit me with such an impact that my whole system blacked out and started to reboot. As my brain started functioning again, I could hear a deafening scream through a long tunnel echoing towards me. "What the hell are you doing, Doc? You wanna get yourself killed as well?" I wanted to reply, but couldn't. I was just gasping for air, completely winded.

Harry looked puzzled as he slowly rolled off me and brushed the snow from his huge, muscular shoulders. "What the fuck? He jumped, Doc! Why?" He peered over the side briefly and shook his head. "I don't understand people. It's impossible...." He peered down again. "Geez, it's a mess," he said, before glimpsing my way. "Sorry, Doc. Are you okay?" He walked my way. "For a second I thought you were gonna jump too."

I slowly rolled onto my side and got into a sitting position. I could feel a couple of cracked ribs on my right, confirming the brute impact of the six-foot-four, 250-pound security guard.

I embraced the pain. Physical pain always confirmed reality. *There is no real pain in dreams; only fear.* And I could feel the reality stinging me. I slowly hunched forward and held onto my knees.

Harry looked over the side again. He offered me a cigarette. I hadn't smoked in eight years, but I sometimes joined the smokers on the roof to escape from the insanity downstairs.

"Looks like you need one, Doc. Do you smoke? I'm sure I've seen you up here."

I took the cigarette. I had always loved the ritual. The gritty slide of paper on paper as it slipped from the pack, the faint whiff of tobacco, the spark and crackle as the little wheel in the lighter rolled. I cupped my hands to shelter the flame from the breeze. The cigarette lit up. I inhaled. The bitterness and revulsion ran like a nauseating shiver down my spine. I heard the little red coal devouring the tobacco and it soothed my ears. I felt the faint heat on the outside of my fingers. A lost friend greeted me, giving me a dry palate. I should've stubbed it out immediately.

Fuck, I am so spineless and weak. I always said that I was one cigarette away from a pack a day. I stared at the glowing tip. The windy chill flowing over the roof bullied the smoke around. Maybe the next draw would taste better. I took a second long drag. My shoulders dropped into acceptance.

Harry sat down next to me. I hoped he would just sit. I did not feel like a conversation. The numbness was all over me. I didn't even think I could talk; my lips were numb, my mouth dead, and my tongue thick.

Kind people are the worst. And Harry was kind. "A real teddy bear," the nurses called him. "He's such a sweetie pie," they'd say.

He glanced at me, then quickly away. I sensed his discomfort. His urge to console me was bubbling up like milk on the stove.

"Wow, man. Doc Michael, jumping. Who'd believe

it? He was such a cool guy." He was shaking his head slowly. I peeked at him. He had puzzled eyebrows, and tears were rolling down his chubby, bearded cheeks. He rubbed his face on his right shoulder to hide them.

"Jip," was all I got out as my Afrikaans mother tongue kicked in reflexively. The lump in my throat was telling me to cry. I tried clearing it, but it kept its choke on me. It wouldn't release. I hated that feeling: the need to cry, but the inability to do so. A dam of tears was stuck in my throat.

Harry's deep voice broke the silence.

"You were like, best friends, weren't you?"

What were we? How could I define what we had?

"More like blood brothers. Yes, we were bound in blood. He used to say our friendship was set in stone ... petrified."

"Huh?"

"Sorry, Harry. I'm drifting off, and it's a long story. Yes, we were very close."

Harry got up and walked back to the edge of the roof. He looked down again and continued to shake his head in disbelief. He gave a slight whistle, like the wind howling around the corner of a house.

"Wow, Doc ... and you saw him go down?"

I felt tremors run from my hands into my shoulders as I started shaking uncontrollably.

"All the way down," was all I could mumble as the floodgates opened in my eyes.

CHAPTER 2

DAY ONE

She woke with a startle. She tried to blink away the darkness, but it remained.

Drowsy and completely disoriented, she wiped away some cobwebs that were stuck to her face.

"What the...?" she mumbled to herself and noticed her speech was slow and garbled, like a drunk's. She tried to sit up, but could not. It took too much effort, and she slumped back, hitting her head on the cold floor. It made a metallic clang.

She was able to turn her head from side to side, and thus she surveyed the darkness. Flashes of memory came back to her. She tried to reconstruct the events. It was her usual evening walk by the river. She recalled a sudden pinch in the arm. A struggle. Extreme drowsiness and powerlessness. Her arms had been duct taped to the armrests of a wheelchair and there had been duct tape over her mouth and eyes, she recalled clearly. She had banged her head as she was rolled into a large vehicle. It must've been a truck or a van.

Then it was all pitch black.

She tried to get up again. This time she propped up her elbows to prevent herself from falling down. She got her breath back, leaned forward, and was able to sit up while supporting herself with her hands on the floor. The floor was ice cold and metallic.

What is this place?

"Help!"

"*Help!*"

"*Please* help me! Get me out of here!"

She yelled till her voice was hoarse. Metallic echoes were the only replies.

She tried to crawl, but her legs still dragged, so she sat there and waited. After a while she tried again. Finally, she felt her legs and had the power to crawl. She crawled forward as quickly as she could and smashed into a steel wall with her face. She tasted blood, rust, and wet metal. She followed the wall and within a few moments reached a corner. *That's about forty feet.* She turned the corner and continued crawling. The second corner arrived much quicker. *Ten feet, maybe?* She crawled down that wall to the third corner.

When the reality hit her, she started to cry. "Oh my God, oh my God, no.... I am in a fucking metal box!"

She found a soft, long object, about a metre long. In the darkness, she figured out it was a rolled-up yoga mat. She was able to roll it out, curl into a fetal position on top and sob herself to sleep.

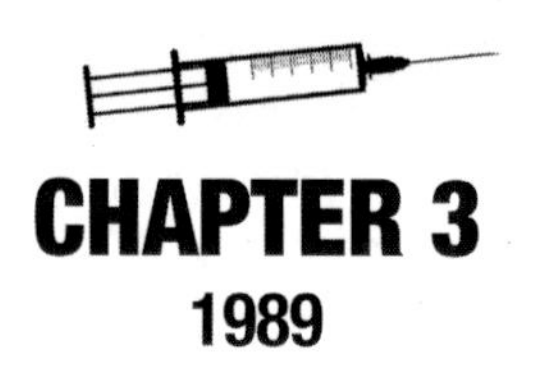

CHAPTER 3

1989

Cape Town, South Africa

"Mr. Benáde, what is the nerve called that wraps around the humerus right here?"

A long pause followed.

The silence hung. All eyes in the dissection room were on me. Professor Ardon was glaring.

I blushed. The flush of blood warmed my ears. Then a cool chill of relief passed through when I realized I knew the answer.

"The axillary nerve!"

Michael Clarke and I answered simultaneously. I looked across the table. Unlike me, he was calm and at ease. His tanned, olive skin did not show any flush. His emerald green eyes were locked on me. At just over six feet, I looked up at him. The professor turned his attention to Michael, but Michael kept his eyes on me. His comforting, warm smile somehow put me at ease, like he was a big brother looking out for me.

"So, Mr. Clarke," the professor continued, "since

you're so keen to save Mr. Benáde here, which muscle does it innervate?"

"The deltoid," Michael shot back, before my brain was even out of the starting block. Michael turned his gaze towards the professor as if to challenge him. His back was straight and his head cocked slightly backwards. It was a stand-off.

Professor Ardon paused and looked at his watch.

"Okay, everyone, let's cover those cadavers and we will see you back here on Tuesday to complete the shoulder dissection."

We pulled the formalin-soaked sheet over our cadavers and packed up. Upon leaving, Michael walked out right behind me. He had never spoken to me until that moment, and his first words caught me off-guard.

"Do you know what separates Batman from all the other superheroes?" he said. I kept walking. I didn't think he was talking to me until I looked over my shoulder and noticed there was no one else. I jerked my head around in surprise.

"Sorry, are you talking to me?"

He smiled and continued talking as he slowly nodded a yes. "Batman doesn't have any superpowers." I halted my next step to allow Michael to walk next to me. He continued to talk to me so comfortably you'd think that we had been friends for years. "Batman is a normal human being, but he uses his intelligence and technological inventions to conquer the villains. He could actually exist."

He stopped, stuck out his right hand. "Hi. I'm Michael Clarke." We shook hands.

"Peter Benáde."

"Want to join me for the new Batman movie tonight? It's the Tim Burton production with Michael Keaton and Jack Nicholson ... got great reviews...."

I wasn't sure, as I had planned to study all evening. "I've never really considered it. I'm not really a super-hero movie guy, but it'll probably be a good break from the books for a night...."

"Oh, you'd love it. I've loved the comics since my dad bought me my first comic books. It's got a lot of symbolism. *Batman* is a modern day parable. The small boy, Bruce Wayne, is left to fend for himself in the cruel dangerous world of Gotham City, where the villain has slain his parents." He talked in an animated, dramatic fashion: rolling his eyes, making grand hand movements, deepening his voice. "The death of his parents is his motivation to create his alter ego, Batman, to conquer evil. He uses his wealth, intellect, science, and technology to fight crime."

This would have been a fascinating bedtime story to a five-year-old. It was filled with drama and suspense as he spoke. "The Bad gave birth to the Good, but our hero is human and he makes mistakes. Through his actions, he creates an even more monstrous villain, the Joker. It's nearly biblical: a troubled angel gets thrown from above and becomes the Joker—the Devil.

"Just like the Devil, the Joker is popular with the people of Gotham City. They don't fear him. They don't see the truth. He exploits their vanities by poisoning their cosmetic products. They die by laughing themselves to death."

Is he ever going to stop?

"It's a glimpse of modern society, isn't it? I don't have to explain it all to you, Peter. It becomes clear as day the moment you think about it as more than a kids' cartoon."

"Okay, okay. With such a sales pitch, I have to go—I'm in."

I did enjoy the movie, and afterwards we had a coffee in Michael's room. He went on and on about the parables, analogies, symbols, and ironies contained in his huge collection of *Batman* comic books.

"I think he's a bit of a loner and a freak," Michael said. "Batman, along with his alter ego, Bruce Wayne, is adored by women, but he can never find love and commitment. Women are his Achilles' heel."

"Then we have one thing in common," I joked. I was beginning to appreciate Batman differently.

"Wait, let me show you my collection!" He jumped up and pulled down a large ring binder from the top of his bookshelf. "You've got to see this artwork of the Joker."

He opened the folder on his lap, and all his comic books were preciously wrapped and chronologically stored in plastic sleeves. He paged through the collection with a meticulous method. He would slide his right hand under the plastic sleeve containing the comic book, then he would place his left hand on the top. Keeping his hands together, as if in prayer, he would turn the page over. When he got to the edition he wanted to show to me, he opened the rings and took the sleeve out, then turned it upside down and allowed the comic book to smoothly slide out onto his right hand. It was like delivering a baby. In fact, I had seen many babies delivered with less care.

"Look at that Joker's smile." He pointed at the comic book cover. "That's the classic sardonic smile isn't it?" He was beaming from ear to ear.

After showing that to me, he replaced the book himself. Not for a moment did I get the impression that he would allow me to touch the comic book. Everyone has his boundaries.

"You look after those comic books very well."

He paused and contemplated the comment, nodding slowly as he looked at the floor.

"It is all my dad left me."

Silence was broken by a holler down the corridor. "Benáde! Peter Benáde—phone call in the foyer!"

Michael walked down with me to the payphones in the foyer of our hostel. The junior on phone duty pointed to the payphone in the corner.

"Hello? Sure, Dad. Sunday lunch at twelve-noon. No, I don't think I will be able to make it for the morning service. I need to study."

I looked over at Michael and rolled my eyes as my father continued to rant about me not going to church. It was the usual: "Your mother gets so upset if you don't attend Communion."

"Mind if I bring a friend on Sunday?" I asked after he calmed down. Michael looked up abruptly and waved 'no' with his hands. I mimed a plea.

"It's Michael Clarke. One of my classmates."

"Yes, Dad, I know you haven't heard his name. I only met him in class this week. No, I don't know actually. Why don't you ask him on Sunday? Noon, then? Okay, love you." I hung up. "Sorry, Michael, but I need a friend to go. Someone they can interrogate besides me."

Michael smiled.

"Sure, sure. I wouldn't mind a home-cooked meal, and I don't mind the questions. Hope they can handle the answers."

On Sunday we drove to my parents' place in Stellenbosch, the heart of South Africa's wine region. It was a beautiful autumn day, with the vineyards painted rusty yellow and brown. As we entered town with its surrounding mountain ranges, I realized again how privileged I was to grow up here. It truly was a hub for education, with excellent schools and a world-renowned university. When you grew up here, there was never a question of whether or not you would go to university; it was only a question of which profession you would choose. I was groomed for it from the first day I put my foot through the school door, especially since Dad was the high school principal. Even when I was a small boy, people questioned me at church: "What are you going to be one day, little Peter? A lawyer? Engineer? A doctor, maybe?" Higher education was everything here. Stellenbosch was the mecca of intellectual snobbism. I could scoff at it, but it drove me to be in medical school. Years later, watching the film *Revolver*, I was struck by Jack Green when he said, "We're approval junkies. We're all in it for the slap on the back and the gold watch. The hip-hip-hoo-fuckin'-rah. Look at the clever boy with the badge, polishing his trophy." That described me to a T.

I drove down the lane of trees to the end of the cul-de-sac and arrived just as my dad was getting out of the car in his church suit. Mom did not join him, probably so she could cook lunch.

I gave Dad a quick hug and noticed his shirt's armpits were soaked with sweat. He had his jacket over his left arm, and he wiped his brow with his cuff as I introduced Michael. "Michael, this is my dad, Cobus."

"Nice meeting you, Mr. Benáde," Michael said. They shook hands.

We entered the front door to be welcomed by the great, familiar aroma of Sunday lunch: oven chicken and baked potatoes. We found my mother in an apron washing her hands in the sink when we entered. "Mom, this is Michael." Michael gave her his warm, stunning smile, which always made the girls in class swoon, and stretched out his hand. My mom ignored his hand and hugged him warmly. "Welcome to our home, Michael. Pieter, your dad's probably getting rid of his tie, so would you open a bottle of wine for us? Look in the fridge in the scullery for what you would like. I presume a cold white would be best on such a warm day. You can add some soda to mine."

My dad returned with his tie gone and a fresh, neat dress shirt on. He walked up to my mom and she turned her cheek for his quick kiss. "Can I cut the meat?" he asked.

"No, it's just chicken, so you can do it by the table. Why don't you men sit in the dining room and I will finish up here."

I poured some Zonnebloem Blanc de Blanc and, as requested, added a bit of soda to my mom's glass.

"Mr. Benáde, Peter tells me you're the principal of Stellenbosch High School. The kids aren't driving you crazy yet?" he teased.

"I think we are lucky in this town as many of their parents are lecturers at the university or involved in education, so many kids are pretty driven. But yes, we have our washouts. Those ones without drive or principles are harder to deal with, but it's the parents' fault, not the kids'. That's how I see it. If a kid gives me trouble, I look at the parent. The successes and failures of children reflect the parenting. Many kids don't have any moral standards any more. We always say, *vroeg ryp, vroeg vrot.* If you're ripe early, you're rotten early. They have sex, fall out of school pregnant, and that's it for their careers. Anyway, it's just getting worse." He paused. "What does your dad do, Michael?"

"My dad died when I was eleven."

"Oh, sorry. I wasn't aware."

"Of course, sir, no problem. Anyway, it's been a

long time since those men in uniform knocked on the door. He died in the Border War. He was a Recce. He wasn't home often, but he always said he did what needed to be done. He was very much a man of principles and rules."

"Did he die in combat?" I looked at my dad in shock for asking.

Michael seemed comfortable with answering. "They just told us it happened during a special mission in Mozambique. I researched it, and there was a lot of reconnaissance work going on during the war at Lourenzo Marques. I think Russian arms were brought in through that port. My dad told me that his unit was made up of very well-trained divers, so I made my own deductions. Some reports say that Special Forces divers would swim up the Limpopo to survey the harbour. Hundreds of casualties of war were actually victims of the crocodiles...."

My dad sat frozen in shock.

"I think it's ironic that my dad probably got killed by a Nile crocodile whilst he was working for the 'Old Crocodile.'"

While he was talking my mother walked into the room and heard Michael's last sentence. She placed the chicken on the table.

"The Old Crocodile! Didn't know you boys even knew about that nickname. Old PW Botha, on the TV every time with that handkerchief in his top pocket. Crocodile tears for the dead boys. I get angry every time I think of that." She shook her head as she reflected.

There was a moment of silence before Michael continued.

"I could never truly confirm how my dad died, but it is more important that he died for the principles he believed in. He won an Honoris Crux during Operation Reindeer in Angola, so I know he was a good soldier. I don't believe in any war, but I respect him for his conviction to follow his beliefs."

My mother looked at Michael. "It sounds like you agree with Gandhi's remark, 'I am prepared to die, but there is no cause for which I am prepared to kill.'"

Michael gave her a warm and kind smile. "I love that quote, but I disagree. You misunderstood me, Mrs. Benáde. I don't like war, but I despise pacifists even more. My dad might have fought a stupid war for a ridiculous cause, but in the end, at least he died for what he believed in. He always said there were many things in this world that needed to be done, but only a few people with the guts to do it." Michael's voice became deep and dramatic. "'Son, you must *be* one of the few that will do what needs to be done.'" He smiled.

"I hear you, Michael, but the question is what needs to be done in this country," my dad weighed in.

"OK. Let us stay clear of the politics today," my mom announced with a smile. "Let's dish up."

As we reached for our utensils, my dad leaned forward and took my mother's hand as well as mine. He closed his eyes. "Let's say grace." He rambled his usual prayer. The words rolled so fast it was pure ritual. The harmony of the words I had known since infancy, but the actual words and meaning I could only distinguish years later. As always, my mother echoed the final "Amen."

We raised our glasses for the customary toast: "Smaaklike ete!" Afrikaans for *bon appétit.* We took our first few bites in silence, and then my mother asked, "Michael, is your mother still alive?"

"Yep."

Silence.

"Does she still live in the Transvaal? I sensed a Johannesburg accent."

Michael seemed slightly amused by my mother's comment. "Impressive, Mrs. Benáde. I did grow up in Jo'burg, but no, she's down here in Cape Town now. She moved to Bellville after my dad's death."

My mother spoke to me. "You should bring her over next time. Everyone's welcome for Sunday lunch."

"She won't come, but thank you for the invitation," Michael said briskly, looking at his plate.

"I would love to meet her...."

Michael looked up at my mother and his face hardened a little bit. "Thank you again, Mrs. Benáde, but she is housebound and will not come. I will extend your invitation." His tone was calm, but very firm. Michael changed the subject immediately. "So, Mrs. Benáde, are you a teacher too?"

"No, I am the librarian at the university library."

"That library always amazes me, being built three stories underground."

"It is impressive, I agree. How they managed to build it underneath the university's centre garden square and keep it so well lit with all those roof windows is fascinating. I love reading and literature, and I find the library ideal for me. Peace, calm, silence, and millions of printed words to choose from."

My mother seemed pleased with how she'd escorted Michael back to the comfort of a normal conversation.

My dad then asked Michael what he thought of the Western Province fly-half performance in the Currie Cup rugby game the day before, and I knew that he liked Michael. By the end of the afternoon Michael had my parents wrapped around his finger. Looks and charm, he had it all.

CHAPTER 4

1990: THE BEACH BOYS

We got the house!" Michael announced as he burst into my room.

"Whoa, whoa, whoa. What house? Who are *we*?"

"Me, you, Danté, and I think Werner Krige is interested. What do you mean, *what house*? The beach house in Blouberg, of course. It's the coolest student house in the world. On the beach in Blouberg strand, crawling distance from the Blue Peter Pub, million-dollar view. I have been talking about it for months!"

"As a distant possibility. Not right now! I didn't even know it was available."

"Well, Greg and his buddies who rented it screwed up one too many times. When you add up their averages for the last semester, the four of them did not even get one hundred per cent. So I think Greg's dad pulled the plug and the landlord was fed up with the monster beach parties on the lawn. Greg was the one who signed the rental agreement. So when I heard that Greg's dad was ripping him out of there, I got hold of the landlord. He is not going to let the other guys take it over. He's basically kicking them out, and I just told him the truth: that I am at the top of the fourth-year class and you're not far behind me. And when I told him Danté played for Maties first team rugby, the deal was done!"

"I'm not sure, Michael. I'm not a natural like you. I have to work hard to get those marks. That place is for the cool party guys."

Michael pulled his shoulders back as if I'd offended him. He pointed at me and then flipped his hands towards his own chest.

"Look at you and me. We're cool! We can pull it off." He smiled. It was obvious he was very excited. "Listen, Peter. I know the place has a reputation, but it is a fantastic opportunity to 'suck the marrow from life,' as they said in *Dead Poets Society*. But no pressure. If you wanna stay in the hostel here, you might keep up your test scores more easily, but life offers so many other forms of scoring at the beach house. I know you well enough to say I think you need this. You need to learn how to live a little. Life happens outside these hospital walls, Peter. Too many doctors' whole existence is defined by their career. Medicine is great and interesting, but it can be like a parasite in your system that sucks you dry from the inside till it kills you. To survive as a human being, you need to see the other side of life ... the side outside medicine. You need to live!"

His excitement was intoxicating. The freedom and opportunities on offer lured me in. I could feel my heart beating faster.

"So, Doc Clarke, if I understand you correctly, you are concerned I might contract this condition called you-have-no-life-except-medicine. You are kindly offering me a vaccination against this boring-life condition. The vaccination is called 'the beach house.'"

"Exactly." Michael smiled.

I felt very sharp and witty.

We moved in the next month and the house-warming party was legendary. As a first-class rugby player and fourth-year medical student, Danté had a group of blonde, beautiful girls who followed him to all the games. They spread the news. It was easy to gather a big crowd of partygoers when you had the ultimate venue: Blouberg Beach. Our beach house had a barbeque going on the front lawn and people arriving for sundowners, only to leave at sunrise the next day. The girls were gorgeous. I had a few beers and tried to make small talk like the other guys.

I approached a bronzed, blonde beauty and tried to be witty by opening with: "You have a beautiful glow to your biggest organ...."

She spun around and then I saw she had huge breasts. "Geez!" she barked and walked away.

"Your skin—I meant your skin! Skin is our biggest organ...." She didn't hear me, so quickly was she trying to escape *the pervert.*

I had had enough of the scene, so I took a couple of beers and walked onto the beach in front of our house. I needed to get out.

Michael walked up and sat down next to me. We

quietly watched the waves rolled in. I looked over my shoulder at the house, the party still going on.

"I don't get it. I don't have the skill you guys have to pick up girls. I don't want to play anymore."

"Peter, you are a blond, attractive guy. I see the way girls look at you. You sell yourself short. Remember this." He turned towards me, took my shoulders in his hands, and turned me until he was looking straight in my eyes. "If you don't believe in yourself, no one else will."

We sat there in silence for a while.

"Are you coming back inside?" he asked.

"Maybe a bit later."

He left me, and I sat for a while admiring the beauty of Big Bay. The ocean always calmed my emotions.

Surprisingly, a petite brunette sat down next to me.

"Hi. I'm Claire. Looks like you're having a tough time at the party. I saw you flee. I hate these scenes as well—my friends dragged me here. Mind if I join you for a bit?"

"Sure."

"Life giving you a hard time? Break-up or something?" she probed.

"Or something...." I replied vaguely, and she presumed the worst.

"Well, I've been there, done that, and sometimes I just want people to give me space and not ask too many questions. Sometimes you just need someone to sit next to you."

For some reason I leaned my head on her

shoulder. She wrapped her arm around my head and laid my head on her lap. Then she scratched the back of my neck and scalp with her nails. Goosebumps of pleasure ran up my spine. We didn't say much more, but she walked me to my room when the party started to die down.

The next morning, she woke up and started to get dressed. I felt a bit guilty for the obvious one-night-stand situation. "Would you give me your number?" I said uncomfortably.

She smiled knowingly and shook her head slowly. "We both know what this was. Fun." She smiled, kissed me on the forehead, and left. No number, no contact details, no guilt.

I pulled on some shorts and walked to the kitchen for coffee.

Danté was the first to comment. "That was a hot little brunette that just slipped out. Well done, Mr. Benáde! Never thought you had it in you. Got her number?"

"No," I said as I blushed.

"One-night stand, then?"

"I think she felt sorry for me."

"And comforted you all night as her good deed?"

I nodded.

"Then she left you to your sorrows in the morning, not wanting to get involved?"

"Sort of," I mumbled.

"That's a spectacular pick-up! What's your secret?" he joked.

"Nothing really. I sat on the beach watching the waves, and she walked over thinking the worst. I leaned my head on her shoulder and she took it from there."

"Geez, Werner," Danté yelled down the hallway. "You should hear Mister-I-am-so-deep-and-thoughtful-head-on-the-shoulder's pick-up story!" He laughed. "High five, Peter," he said and walked to Werner's room.

Michael entered the kitchen with a knowing smile on his face. As he walked towards the coffee machine, he placed his hand on my shoulder and gave it a quick squeeze. Great friendships are moulded by the unsaid. He looked out the window as the coffee percolated.

"The swell looks good. Let's go surfing."

Our life was filled with special surprises, like the day the *Scope* ladies came over. In 1990, the South African government had strong censorship restrictions. Pornography was strictly banned, and the laws governing it were strongly enforced in South Africa. Men were starved for it, and there was a huge commotion any time a fellow student got their hands on a *Playboy* smuggled in from overseas. *The Scope* men's magazine was the South African version of its overseas counterparts. The pictures were all very soft porn. All the girls wore panties and had little stars printed over their nipples. Those pictures needed to be taken somewhere, and how lucky we were with our location at the Beach House. On a bright summer's day, we walked out of our house to find a magazine photo shoot of two stunningly beautiful blonde sisters, right on our doorstep. Gobsmacked and drooling with lust, we sat watching this beautiful exhibition of female nudity, with no little stars to obstruct our view. For Michael, watching wasn't enough. He needed to get closer and "better inspect these perfect examples of the female anatomy." He slipped into his tight-fitting Speedo bathing suit and calmly walked into the photo shoot as if he were a male model. He marched right past the security guard, who was trying to keep a perimeter with all the men ogling away at the boobs on display. Michael fit in like a glove, a tanned six-foot-two Adonis standing between two blondes like a Greek god with two angels by his side. Before anyone else caught on who he was, he lightly pinched one girl's butt cheek and whispered something in the ear of the other. They both blushed and sneaked a peek at his butt as he turned and walked into the ocean. Werner, Danté, and I were high-fiving each other, incredulous that our housemate could be so cool. Danté and Werner went clubbing in Cape Town that evening. Michael and I were having a whiskey on the porch when a taxi pulled up and, to my surprise, the blonde twins got out. They joined us for a few drinks.

At some point during the conversation, Michael said, "Listen, girls, I don't mean to be rude, but your bodies are way more attractive than any piece of clothing you can cover them with." They just smiled, stood up, and flicked the thin shoulder straps of their light summer dresses to make them fall to the floor. Calmly they sat down again and continued the conversation in complete nudity. No inhibitions—what a revelation.

CHAPTER 5

DAY 2

She woke, still lying in the fetal position on the yoga mat. It wasn't complete darkness anymore.

On the far side of the box, she could see light piercing through a sliver of a crack by the door hinge. She was able to get up. All power had returned to her limbs and most of the drowsiness was gone. *I must've been drugged last night.* She walked to the sliver of light. It was clear now that she was trapped in a large metal shipping container. When she peered through the small opening, she could only see trees and forest. She twisted her head and listened acutely. There were no cars or city sounds, only the terrible silence of nature.

She turned her back to the doors and looked into the darkness. With the light behind her, she could see the far wall most clearly. She slowly slid down to her haunches. *Holy fuck.*

"Matthew 7:7," a digitally distorted voice announced loudly, and it echoed through the metal. She nearly peed herself as she jumped from the fright. It came from a speaker mounted in the roof. The voice spoke artificially slow to make the distortion worse.

"Ask and you shall receive."

Her initial scare was replaced with a burst of anger.

"*Get* me out of here! Open the door!" she yelled. "You said, 'Ask'! I am asking! Open the door. Open the door! Let me go."

"That is not what you asked for," the voice replied.

"What do you mean? Who the hell are you? Let me go! *Please*."

The voice did not reply. The static from the speaker disappeared.

"Hello, are you still there?"

Silence.

"*Hey! Hello!*"

Silence.

She started to bang the walls with her hands. She kicked and screamed and smashed the wall to make as much noise as she possibly could. When she ran out of steam, she let out a final loud yell. "*No, God!*"

She looked at her bleeding hands in the blade of daylight that passed through the box.

The voice spoke again.

"This is your second chance. You were not successful the first time. This time you will be."

"What?"

"There is no escape. No one knows you are here. Here is nowhere. It's simple: Complete the task and be set free."

"What the fuck are you talking about?" she yelled.

"In time it all will be revealed. Go to the light," the voice replied.

"Or what?" She hollered defiantly.

"*Die!*" The voice thundered, so loud that it stunned her and she dropped to the floor grabbing her ears. The metal echoed and her ears rang for a few seconds thereafter.

Oh my God.

In the furthest corner a spotlight came on and blasted a circle of light to the floor. She walked over and stood underneath it, still trembling.

"Do not leave the circle of light. If you do, you will *die* here in this box in the middle of nowhere. One step outside of that circle, and it is over. Do you understand?"

She nodded quietly.

"Good," the voice said.

Shit, there must be a camera in here. An ice-cold shiver of fear trickled up her spine. She looked around the roof but could not see it. It was too dark, and those cameras could be minute.

The voice continued.

"The hatch will open now. Do not leave the circle of light. Do you understand? Speak."

"Yes."

With a load clang she heard something unlock in the roof. On the opposite end of the room a small hatch opened, and through it two large, flat crates with packs of bottled water were lowered. She could hear a chain whir through a gear system. From her angle she could not see a person. On the crates of bottled water were a shoebox and a large plastic container. The plastic container had a lid with a hole in it the size of a dinner plate. Next to the container was a roll of toilet paper.

As soon as this touched the floor, the chain unhooked and disappeared into the roof again. The hatch slammed shut. Footsteps on the roof. She could hear a creaking ladder.

The light switched off and the circle of confinement was gone.

The voice spoke again.

"Do your bodily functions in the plastic container. Leave the container under the hatch, and it will be emptied. It is simple. Do you understand?"

"Yes," she whimpered.

Looking at the setup, she realized that every detail had been accounted for.

The voice had a last mantra. This sounded different; like a recording.

"You asked and you shall receive.

"Drink the water.

"Cherish the food.

"Use the body function container.

"It's that simple."

She stayed in the corner, because the tremors of fear did not allow her to move. She sat down and felt a sharp object poke her butt. She felt around for it. It was a small screw. She picked it off the floor and walked to the wall still illuminated by the sliver of light.

She scratched two short vertical lines on the wall.

Day 2. September 17, 2011.

CHAPTER 8

1991: REALITY CHECK

The payphone by the corner of our property kept ringing. We did not have a phone in our house, so we would give out the payphone on the street corner as our contact number. When it rang for the fourth time, I ran from my room to answer it.

"Yes, hello?" I expected someone to say *wrong number* as usual.

"Is Mickey there?" It was a very high-pitched voice.

"There is no Mickey here."

I was about to put the phone down when she said, "Are you sure? Michael Clarke? I'm his mother."

"Sorry, Mrs. Clarke. I am Peter Benáde, Michael's friend. I wasn't aware you called him Mickey. No, he isn't here. Can I take a message?"

"Oh, could you?" I didn't think her voice could go any higher but it pitched into a screech. "Please tell him Jared is sick and I need him to come over right away. When will he be in?"

"I guess he'll be back soon. Is there anything that

I—" the phone call was disconnected and a dial tone rang in my ear. I looked at the mouthpiece. She had hung up.

Michael was skydiving. When he walked into the house I called out, "Mickey!" in the highest voice I could master. He snapped, dropped all his gear, and rammed me into the wall so hard that the whole house shook. His face was right up in mine, and our noses touched.

"Don't ever call me that."

I held my hands up in self-defence, and my eyes begged for forgiveness.

"Whoa, man! Why so touchy?"

"What does she want?" he snapped at me.

"I don't know. She said Jared or someone is sick and you need to come over. She put the phone down too quickly for me to ask anything. Gee, Michael. I was only teasing you a bit, man. I'm sorry."

He took a long, deep breath and let it slide out slowly.

"I'm the one that has to apologize. Sorry. Just when I think I'm free, she drags me back in."

He grabbed his car keys and started to walk out. He stopped and turned.

"Peter, would you drive with me?"

He did not say a word during the drive there. We pulled up to a tiny house in one of the less affluent areas of Bellville. A chain-link fence bordered a small front yard of un-mowed grass. We got out, and Michael ripped out a plastic grocery bag that was stuck in the fence and shoved it in his pocket. He unlocked the front door and yelled inside. "Mom, I'm here. I brought Peter with me."

A high-pitched voice came from the living room. "Oh, Mickey, you know I don't like strangers!"

"Mom. He's my friend. You spoke with him today, for God's sake. Stop being so paranoid."

I entered the house and immediately noticed a strangely pungent smell—a thick, sweaty, fruity feet smell. In the foyer was a picture of Michael's dad in uniform with the Honoris Crux. I walked into the living room and then I saw her.

Holy shit.

I stopped in the doorway. She filled the three-seater couch she was sitting on, from side to side. Her tree-trunk sized legs, with the fat billowing over her ankles like jelly, protruded below the sheet of clothing that covered her. Her head appeared artificially small, like a golf ball stuck on a watermelon, but she had a friendly smile.

"Hi, Peter. Nice to meet you."

I was digesting the shock. Dumbstruck.

Michael spoke. "What's with Jared? I pay him, you know. Couldn't one of the other Jehovah's come to help?"

"He is sending a friend tomorrow. Don't be so rude! They're so good to me. I just need you to help me quickly" —she looked at me and changed her voice to a whisper— "with you know what, and maybe you can hand me the TV remote. I dropped it." She pointed where it lay on the floor, three feet away from the couch.

Michael looked at me. Disgust and anger was all I saw in him.

"Peter, would you give us a moment?"

I walked out of the house, but not quick enough. I heard his mother say, "Michael, put the pot right in the middle under me, you know, through the back of the couch, there. Quick, hurry up. I can't hold it any more."

I stayed outside. My mother would criticize me for having bad manners by not greeting her when we left, but I could not step back inside that place. I was horrified that someone could live like that. I felt sorry for her, but on the other hand I could not stomach going back in there.

When Michael walked out I could see a shiver of revulsion run up his spine. He appeared gaggy and stopped at the 7-Eleven for a can of ginger ale.

"She wasn't always a beached whale."

Boy, that's a harsh thing to say about your mother. How do I reply to that? I didn't.

After a few minutes he started to talk. "The Jehovah's actually saved me. I was her main caregiver when she could still shuffle around a bit. She was paranoid of strangers. I couldn't get anyone else to care for her because she was scared of black domestic workers. Jared rang the bell regularly to spread his message, and suddenly one day, he wasn't a stranger anymore. I employed him and his Jehovah friends to take care of Mom as their special church outreach project. She actually needs a care home, but she won't go." Silence hung in the car so he turned on the radio just in time for the news:

"Gang wars are again occurring on the Cape Flats. It has been reported that a fight broke out between the vigilante group PAGAD, the People Against Gangsterism And Drugs, and one gang named The Firm. Police were sent to secure the area, and the police spokesperson said at the news conference that rubber bullets were used to break up the fight. Currently our news crews are not allowed into the area, so we will report as soon as more information is available. The turnoff to Langa from the N2 has been barricaded and we suggest you avoid the area on your commute home."

Michael looked over at me. "Man, Africa is not for sissies. Sounds like a bloodbath on the Flats." He turned the radio off. "Maybe a good night to go to trauma. There will be lots to do. Probably a few good stabbings for chest drains and stuff."

I nodded. "Not a bad idea. I should do that."

Those violent Saturday nights were the best way to gain a lot of experience with practical medical skills like suturing wounds, splinting fractures, placing chest drains, and managing gunshots and stabbings. We were medical voyeurs, eagerly watching our peers drag dead people back to life, while we were expected to do the "little" procedures, the ones the seniors were fed up with. "See one, do one, teach one," was the motto. Sink or swim.

I smelled blood and cleaning solution as I walked down the green, echoing hallway towards the trauma department a few hours later. I was armed only with my stethoscope (which I never used in there) in my white coat pocket. A nervous wreck, but all dressed up with a tie and shiny shoes, as expected of all medical students.

I passed the resuscitation area and peeked in. It was utter chaos. Nurses scurrying to and fro, doctors yelling orders, and blood everywhere. I overheard one nurse comment to the matron, "Those bullets look pretty real to me." She pointed to the x-ray film up on the light box in the trauma room. She got an order barked in her direction and ran down the hallway towards the blood bank.

I looked back at the x-ray; even I could clearly see the bright spots where the patient's chest and abdomen were riddled with lead. I recalled the official police statement I heard on the radio driving to the hospital. *The police used no live ammunition to subdue an uprising in one of the Cape Flats townships.* But those weren't rubber bullets; it was live ammunition if I ever saw it. I knew governments lied to the public all the time, but there I stood, witness to tangible proof.

The nurse returned from the blood bank. She was running towards the resuscitation room with a fresh supply of blood. The matron turned towards her and yelled, "Jy kamma loop! Dis als kla!"

You can walk. It is all over.

Latex gloves snapped and protective gowns

dropped onto the floor. Everyone stepped away from the bed. A few shook their heads slowly in thought as they looked at the young boy on the table in front of them. Everyone looked down, except for the trauma team leader. He looked up at the back wall and said, "TOD: twenty-one oh five. Thanks, people. We gave it our best shot."

As I entered through the rubber swinging doors of the trauma unit, the mixed smell of blood, cheap alcohol, and fruity feet hit me full in the face. I felt my shoe sticking to the floor. Looking down, I found I stood in a large puddle of blood.

It was a war zone. I couldn't even identify the doctors initially. A charge nurse or matron rushed past me and grabbed my sleeve. She pulled me up to a bleeding patient, let my sleeve go, and yelled as she scooted further down the hallway to the trauma code in process, "Moenie hier rondstaan nie boetie. Doen iets!" *Don't just stand around, young boy. Do something.*

I looked at 'my patient' not knowing what to do at all. On the bed next to him was another trauma victim getting a chest drain for hemothorax—blood in the chest cavity. He was writhing and didn't appear fully anesthetized. Someone held his one arm up while they got to work on his chest. When the chest drain entered the chest, an arc of blood as thick as my finger shot out and the doctor—or student—doing the procedure jumped out of the way. The blood shot right across the room and covered my neat shoes in red goo. It was the last thing I saw. Everything became pixelated and then black.

I opened my eyes to see a crowd of faces looking down at me. "He's okay," someone said, and then they all dispersed to their duties. Some giggled and one nurse said, "Wooo, 'n groentjie!" *I was a green newbie.* How embarrassing. Fainting in a puddle of blood in the middle of the trauma unit. As soon as I realized what had happened, I jumped up in the hope of minimizing my embarrassment, but of course, everyone had already seen it. Worst of all, I made eye contact with one of the cockiest guys in our class, Stephen Halstead: intelligent, but a real self-centred ass.

Sometimes you meet someone and, for no particular reason, you hate his guts instantly. He was that guy. Always trying to ask the clever questions, always a little niggle when he corrected someone else, always that little bit of condescension in his voice. "Wait, let *me* show you how to do that *properly....*" Ass. Of all the people in the world, why did he have to be the one to witness my failure? A wry, patronizing smirk spread across his face as his eyes taunted me: *I saw you faint. Nah nah nah nah nah.* I wanted the earth to swallow me.

I quickly snuck into the hallway to "get some air," slipped out of the hospital, and drove back home. Humiliated. Feeling green and nauseous. I thought I'd never be able to do the job. Maybe I didn't have the right stuff. I felt like a homeless person with Alzheimer's wandering the streets. Lost. Hopeless. Aimless. I dare say useless. *If I couldn't be a doctor, what could I be?* My mind spun. I needed to talk to Michael urgently. He was always good at helping me gain some insight and perspective.

Arriving at home, I barged into Michael's room. He was lying on his back in bed, his head and shoulders propped up on a couple of pillows against the wall. The room was dark with the moonlight coming through the small window. Michael was slowly smoking a cigarette, and the red glow of its tip illuminated his face. He appeared to be deep in thought, looking out at the ocean.

"Hi, Michael. I had the worst night ever. The trauma room was chaos and I had to suture this one guy, but next to him they were placing a...."

The bed covers around his groin moved, and a blonde head of hair popped out, saying, "Do you mind?"

That's how I met Sandra le Grange.

"Shit, I should've known better!" I yelped and quickly closed the door.

I walked to the beach to catch some air.

To my surprise, I saw the blonde slowly strolling out towards me on the beach. I didn't expect her. Maybe Michael, but not the girl. She was wearing only a very loose-fitting, white, cotton shirt. It was one of Michael's 'pirate shirts.' They were a fashion fad at Cape Town Green Market Square. The shirt just about covered all the essentials, but I could not take my eyes off her beautifully slim, tanned legs. A loose curl of blonde hair fell down to her chest. She floated onto the beach like angel. Her curvy walk had a sleek, catlike rhythm to it. She dragged her feet, and each step made a beautiful *whoop* sound caused, they say, by the silica in the sand. The friction ignited faintly glowing phosphorous streaks. It was a mystical vision.

She was simply the most beautiful woman I had ever seen.

As she sat down next to me, she pulled her knees up to her chest and tucked them under the loose shirt.

I apologized again. "Sorry for barging in on you guys."

She had a comforting laugh. "Don't worry, we're just messing around. It's all fun."

We sat there for a while staring out over the ocean. Rogue waves were hitting the rocky shoreline in front of the hotel. They ricocheted back into the sea, causing huge splashes as they collided with the waves rolling in.

"The sea is restless," she said.

"It *is*."

"Michael says you're a seriously solid guy ... whatever that means."

"He's a great buddy."

"I don't know any *seriously solid* people, so I thought I'd say hi."

She formally stuck out her hand and her stunning, crystal blue eyes looked through me.

"I'm Sandra."

"I am Pieter Benáde; my friends call me Peter." I

shook her hand nervously. "Actually, the name on my birth certificate is the historic family first name: Petrus. My parents are Afrikaans so they call me Pieter. Some Afrikaans guys call me Pieta, but in English it turns into Peter...." *Aaagh. Awkward!* I felt so nervous. *Stop babbling on.*

"Just call me Peter."

"Okay, Peter it is."

The sea breeze pushed a whiff of her scent in my direction. I felt drunk. My head was swimming in hormones.

"Thanks for checking in on me, Sandra, but I think I'm okay."

She smiled a cunning smile and purposefully bumped her shoulder against mine as she got up. She wiped the sand off her backside.

"You're way more than okay, Peter Benáde. You're interesting. And serious," she mocked. "See ya!" She literally danced off the beach in long swoopy strides.

I sat there in the afterglow. My heart was still racing. I felt truly alive.

The north-western, an onshore breeze, was picking up. It would push the waves down. I knew there would be no surf the next day.

CHAPTER 7

1992: BATMAN RETURNS

Sandra entered our lives like she entered a room: with impact. She loved attention, and brought energy and fun to any occasion. Her smile sexy and her eyes bright, she was always entertaining and exciting. She bloomed when attention focused on her. At our parties, she was right in the centre of the group, and everyone else was somehow under her spell. Whenever she walked in, she'd strike a pose. She'd put her arms above her head, with her wrists upwards and flopped open, and tilt her pelvis forward slightly to show off her great curves and sensual smile, like a showgirl getting a standing ovation. Confidently she'd announce, "Hi, everyone, I am here!" She loved talking with her hands. Her hands were like animated extensions of her voice, flowing with its rhythm. In conversation she spoke more with her body than with words. She would always move and flow, closer and further, leaning in and sitting back, touching your arm or whispering in your ear. She ignored everyone's personal space, but I never saw anyone mind. Michael nicknamed her Catz, because she purred in response to attention when she needed it, but ignored it when she wasn't in the mood.

Although the three of us became good friends, Sandra would still intermittently overnight in Michael's room.

I knew it wasn't supposed to bug me.

About two months after meeting her, I sat on the porch one night. I was sipping on a late-night whiskey in the darkness. The ocean reflected the full moon. Michael and Sandra were messing around in the kitchen, and I wasn't in the mood for it. Sandra's intoxicating laughter echoed down the hallway. I couldn't make out what it was all about, but from the porch I could clearly see the door to Michael's room. At some point he entered his room, and I knew Sandra would probably follow soon. I was holding my breath as she was walked towards his room, but as she reached his doorway, she paused. Her sleek left hand went up to the doorpost to halt her momentum. She stood there in the doorway for a few moments, as if she could feel the weight of my stare on her shoulders. Sandra slowly looked towards the darkness of the porch. Her eyes squinted, and when she finally saw me, she threw her head back to allow all her blonde locks to fall onto her back, almost as if she was waving at me. She calmly continued into Michael's room, but a second later, she re-emerged with her jacket in her hand. She blew a kiss to Michael, and I could hear her say, "No, don't worry. Peter will walk me home."

Michael replied, "Is he still here? I thought he'd gone to the beach?"

I started to walk her to her flat, which was just around the corner from our place.

"Don't you want to go to the beach first?" she asked, already turning that way. We sat down on a part of the beach that was mostly covered with round pebbles.

"What is it about the sea that fascinates you the most?" she asked.

I had to think. "There is a theory that 4.5 billion years ago, a planetary body called Theia smashed into Earth. The impact fused them into one, but nearly destroyed Earth. It left lots of debris, and this eventually formed the moon. We know there is a special cosmic relationship between the moon and Earth. The moon determines the ebb and flow of the ocean; the moon controls its emotions, like a love affair...." She looked intrigued. "Stop me if I get too weird." She smiled and her rolling hand urged me to continue.

I picked up a pebble and gave it to her. "Feel how smooth it is. All the roughness of the rock has been rinsed away by the ebb and flow of the tides. Persistence and time have left a smooth pebble here on the beach. That smoothness you feel represents a bond created by an impact 4.5 billion years ago. That fascinates me. True bonds. Persistence. Time."

"You read all of that into the smoothness of a pebble?"

"I'm always connecting the dots."

"And all I wanna do is smell the salty air and feel

the cool sea breeze on my face!"

"That's amazing. You truly live in the moment, then."

She smiled. "It's all we have."

We listened to the rush of the waves over the pebbles and later I walked her home. She hugged me at her front door and sent me on my way.

Sandra never slept in Michael's room again.

Our trio once hiked to a famous nudist beach called Sandy Bay. I was quite self-conscious, but Michael and Sandra, like the true carefree exhibitionists they were, dropped every shred of clothing on the edge of the beach and pranced around as if there was absolutely nothing out of the ordinary to be seen. The inflation created by such a vision of Sandra could not be hidden or ignored. When she noticed, she flitted up to me and kindly whispered in my ear, "You flatter me, Peter. Let's go for a swim." Any Capetonian can confirm: the ocean temperature around Sandy Bay defies any erection, and thus I was saved.

After a great day on the beach, we went for sundowners in Camps Bay. I felt a great summer glow on my skin. Sandra was gorgeous as always, and this didn't go unnoticed by the group in the corner, among them Stephen Halstead. He always thought he was God's gift to women, but he'd had a few drinks on board and was even more arrogant than usual.

When he came over, I thought that he wanted to gain an introduction to the stunning woman with us, but to my surprise, he said, "Sandra le Grange! Great to see you here in Cape Town! You look stunning."

"Hi, Stephen. Still hitting on every girl you lay your eyes on?" she retorted.

"Oh no. Only the most gorgeous ones!" he laughed. "How long has it been? School prom? Come to think of it, you didn't want to go with me. I think we need to make up for that. Let's go out for dinner and catch up properly, without these two bozos." He was laughing and pointing at Michael and I.

"Here's my number. Give me a call." He wrote his number on a napkin and wanted to hand it to her.

She did not lift her hands and left him hanging with the napkin in his hand, so he placed it on the table. She flashed her most stunning smile and put her arms around the two of us. Pulling us both closer to her sides, she said in her typically animated tone, "You know, Stephen, I'm gonna pass on that one. I actually love these guys. Michael makes me laugh, and Peter is my super solid guy. I've got everything I need. So thanks, but no thanks. Ta-ta." She shooed him off with a gracious but firm wave of her hand, took the napkin, and crumpled it into a paper ball. "The clock is running out! She aims, she shoots...." She threw the napkin ball at the garbage bin in the corner and hit it. "She scores!" She threw her arms in the air. "The crowd roars!"

I beamed.

About two weeks later we took a drive to go watch the whales near Hermanus. They would come close to the shore in Walker Bay, one of the world's best land-based whale watching spots. On the drive there we crossed a bridge over the Palmiet River. Michael pulled over, and we all got out and walked to the bridge.

"Let's jump!"

I assessed the challenge. The jump was at least twelve feet high into the unpredictable brown river of mountain water below.

"I don't know. It's crazy, Michael!"

I looked at Sandra. She had covered her eyes with her hand and was shaking her head from side to side.

Michael walked up to the side. He scratched a cross on the concrete with a rock, after he had taken a long look over the edge. Then he calmly stood on the "x" and jumped. He hit the water with a huge splash and swam to the edge of the river. Then he hollered up to me. "Come on, Peter! You can do it! Just jump from the mark!"

Everything in me told me that it was a bad idea. *Shit, this is very high. What if you hit something? You could break something. You can't see what's underneath the surface. What if…?*

"Stop being a control freak. Just let it go!" Michael yelled.

I huddled on the 'x.' As I leaned back, preparing to jump into the unknown, Michael called out again.

"Peter! You have got to go long! Trust me! Buddy, I am serious, give it all you have. Go long!"

I took a big step back to gain extra momentum and jumped forward with all my power. I anxiously hung in the air forever, flapping my arms wildly in an attempt to stay upright. *Boom.* I broke the surface and sank deep into the brown depths. Air bubbles led me back to daylight, and I surfaced safely. Exhilaration!

Fuck, I did it!

"Yeah!" Michael yelled.

I looked back at the bridge to see Sandra giving me two thumbs up. Sometimes you just need a little nudge to achieve things that you never deemed possible for yourself. However, two years later, when a kid paralysed himself when he hit an invisible concrete pillar foundation under the bridge, I shuddered at the blind trust I had invested in my friend Michael on that day.

As was customary by then, we joined our Batman fanatic, Michael, for the screening of the new movie, *Batman Returns*. But on the drive home, Michael was uncharacteristically quiet as I chatted with Sandra.

"Man, Danny de Vito was great as the Penguin."

"He was so gross, but excellent," Sandra agreed. "I felt like I could smell the fish—that's how gross he was."

"And the black ink ooze. I loved it. What're your thoughts, Michael? You're usually the one ranting and raving."

"It was okay."

Sandra looked perplexed.

"You didn't like it?"

"Would you just let it be, Catz? I said it was okay."

Sandra lifted her eyebrows and shrugged. "Well 'okay,' then."

It was a silent drive home.

The next morning, Michael was late for our ride to the university. I banged on the door. “Michael! We’ve got to go! Danté is driving today and he has lab first thing this morning.”

He didn’t answer. I banged on the door a few more times. I tried it and found it locked.

“Just go!” he hollered. We left for class.

Three days later he came out for a coffee.

“Michael, is there something you want to discuss? You got me worried here.”

“Thanks, Peter. Dark side of the moon. I’ll be back soon.”

He walked back into his room and calmly closed the door.

Two days later, I answered the payphone. I listened as the police officer talked, and then I walked over to Michael’s room.

“Michael, open the fucking door,” I said. The door opened immediately, as if he was standing right there.

“I am so sorry, Michael.” *Life always kicks us when we’re down.* “Your mother was found dead.” He stood expressionless. I wrapped my arms around him and gave him a hug. “They think she had a pulmonary embolism. Jared found her.”

He took in a breath and released it. He leaned back against the doorframe and slid down to his haunches. He put his head in his hands.

“Fuck. It’s over.” He took another deep breath in and out. “It’s gonna be tough to get her out of there.”

“You stay here. I will get it organized.”

It was one of the harder things I had ever arranged. She died in the position she was in when I had met her, sitting on that couch. She wouldn't fit through a normal doorway, and we ended up taking out the living room window while a team of men with two gurneys got her to the crematorium.

After the funeral Michael's energy returned and he gained a new lease on life. "The only responsibility I have left is to live life to the fullest. As Robin Williams said in *Dead Poets Society*, 'Carpe diem. Seize the day. Make your life extraordinary.'"

Always an adrenaline junkie, Michael became even more fearless. In surfing, in running, in biking, in paragliding, and even in medicine, he became invincible. He started pushing everything to the limit.

CHAPTER 8

1993:LAYLA

Werner stormed through the house, mumbling.

"What the hell's going on?" Danté asked.

"Layla is a freaking prostitute!" Werner shouted. Layla lived round the corner from us. "I mean, you know, we've been seeing each other for a bit, and then I saw all these different cars pulling in and out of there at strange times. So I asked her what it was about, and she calmly nodded and said she was an escort. I told her I am not the fucking gambling type, and she smiled at me."

"Is that how you left her? Those were your words?" Danté asked.

"Jip."

Danté shook his head. "You're such an asshole, Werner. You've been having a great time with her, every time. She's been nothing but nice to you, and she's bloody honest. I'm not saying you should have sex with her, but you were friends. You're being an asshole."

Werner did eventually apologize to her when his emotions settled, and they remained friends, but without the benefits. She had an interesting life as a high-end escort. Her day job as a receptionist was a smokescreen to keep the police and the taxman at bay, but her main income was tax-free cash, keeping those night-time visitors happy. Nearly all her regulars were married, and she only took on new customers "on recommendation."

About a month after Werner's hissy fit, Layla came over for a barbeque, so we had the opportunity to delve into her world.

"Don't you feel guilty about what you do?" I asked her. "I mean, you could be wrecking marriages, breaking up families."

"No! No guilt. The truth is this: if a guy is married, and he calls me, either the marriage is a wreck already, which has nothing to do with me, or the marriage has a void. If I fill that void, he goes home satisfied to his loving wife and kids. I am not a home wrecker by any means. If anything, I am a marriage saviour." She laughed and contemplated my statement for a few moments. "Escorts get a bad rap for creating sexual liaisons or being 'home wreckers,' as you said, Peter," Layla continued, "but the true home wreckers are those affairs with the nurse or the receptionist. Those quickies with the office staff quickly become affairs, and those women aspire to become replacements for your wife. For them it's not just sex; they have ulterior motives. Next thing you know, your marriage is on the rocks. I fill a specific physical void. I don't want his love; he doesn't want mine. He wants sex, not love. It's contractual. Yes, it can be fun, and if they do return it's not for love. In fact, if they do fall in love and start getting all clingy, freaky and shit, I cut them off."

"Just like that," Werner blurted out.

Layla smiled and gave him a wink. "I honestly believe every relationship has its voids or incompatibilities. We all start out young, lusty, and horny. Passion oozes from all our glands and then people get married...."

Michael topped up her glass of red wine.

"Thanks, Michael," she said with a smile. "But the old couples you see walking down the beach don't have that juvenile lust and passion anymore. They have something even more special: a lifelong experience of friendship and companionship."

She held out her hands and moved them up and down like the two ends of a scale.

"Love is like a see-saw. On the one end of life you have the passionate youth, filled with lust and energy, and on the other end is old age, with a need for contentment, friendship, and companionship.

"Marital problems occur at this tipping point, because people reach it at different ages. Some men stay lustful until they die, and I know women who never really wanted the sex in the first place. They crossed over to the other side—needing companionship, rather than sex—at a young age. I think it's the main cause for a mid-life crisis. During these turbulent times, when it becomes tiresome for both parties, I get the phone call."

We all sat silently, absorbing her worldly knowledge.

"What I find strange is that women somehow want men to be different from the way they are. It's poor logic. Women successfully lure men in with oestrogen, but then they turn the sex off and expect everything to stay the same. Duh. Men are primal beings. They are programmed to seek the oestrogen and sex and will never change. It's just the way you guys are. It's the bees and the flowers. Flowers attract bees with their nectar. It is crazy for the flower to expect that the bee would stay if there was no more nectar."

She had us pegged. *Maybe men are still Neanderthals, with less hair.*

Michael finally commented. "I envy you for seeing the dark side of everyone. The truth behind their façade."

Layla's eyes lit up, as if Michael knew exactly what she was all about. She sat up and leaned towards him, making intense eye contact. She placed her hand on Michael's thigh. "You wouldn't believe it. The world is not what it appears to be."

Layla's perspectives were foreign to me. In my mind, they were the mere rationalizations of a hooker.

CHAPTER 9

1993: THE PEBBLE

Sandra was very flirtatious with Michael. There was always lots of physical contact between them, but in a fun and playful way. In contrast, Sandra kept her flirtations with me more toned down.

She would jokingly confront me about my attitude of "ownership." According to her, I harboured a strong desire to own certain things before I could enjoy them—to have exclusivity.

"Why don't you just enjoy life, without trying to own it? Like enjoying the beach without feeling the need to own a beachfront property."

It was an easy statement for her to make with her free-spirited personality. I tried to be more free thinking, but sometimes you need to accept who you are. You have to make peace with certain parts of your personality, because they will never change. I wanted exclusivity when it came to certain things. Sandra was one of them.

When I could not hold it in any longer, I pounded

on Sandra's apartment door late one night. She opened with a quizzical expression and rubbing her eye with her fist. I shushed her before she could say anything. "I know it's late, but we need to talk. It's very important."

I took her hand and walked her to the beach in her light, silky nightgown.

It would have been difficult to miss the overwhelming influence of the Dutch courage I had been seeking all afternoon while I sat on the porch drinking beer. In other words, I was drunk.

"Peter, I think I know what this is about. Please don't—"

I put her hand on my lap and opened it. In it I placed the smoothest pebble I had ever found. It was perfect.

"You are my Theia," I said. "From the moment you smashed into my life, things changed forever. You are my moon. You make my emotions ebb and flow, and only you can change this rough rock into a smooth pebble."

"That is beautiful, Peter, but—"

"Will you marry me, Sandra?" I blurted. The words hung there, impossible to retract, for what seemed like forever. The silence killed me.

She slowly slid her thumb over the smoothness of the pebble and then she closed her hand over it. Her eyes had a deep blue tint as she studied my face. She looked down after a few moments and drew a heart in the sand with her finger. Eventually she looked up at the ocean and whispered.

"No, Peter." She paused. "I love you, but ... no. It's too serious, too soon." She kissed my forehead and slowly walked off the beach.

I hated that she was right.

By the end of the week, her dad, a plastic surgeon in Pietermaritzburg, had bought her a ticket to London.

And just like that she was gone.

Michael moved on without a hitch. He amazed me. No regrets. No anger. Taking life as it was handed to him. I know he must've missed her too, but he never seemed to look back. He seemed so unattached, embodying Edith Piaf's "Non, je ne regrette rien."

Unlike me. I regretted everything. I'd ruined it all with my confession. Did I really need to "own" her so badly that I'd sacrifice knowing her altogether? Stupid. Regret.

The last time we heard from Sandra that year was after graduation.

As we were packing up at the beach house, the mailman delivered a postcard. It was a picture post-card taken in a restaurant. Sandra was the glamorous central feature; I expected nothing less. She radiated beauty in her spectacular glittering dress; surrounded by a large group of transvestites all dressed up like Vegas showgirls. On the table lay a menu: 'ODD FELLOWS, 1 Queen Street, Blackpool.'

On the back of the postcard she wrote,

Congrats my Lovies.
Take care of each other!
Love U! Miss U!
I'm having a ball! (ha ha)
xxx
Love
S
AKA Catz!

CHAPTER 10

DAY 5

Hunger woke her. It was very early; the light was just starting to slip in. Her stomach had been rumbling for the last two days—she had never felt so hungry. She felt dizzy upon getting up. The shoebox had three airline-sized packets of cashew nuts and almonds and three bananas in it. She finished that in twenty minutes, and since it had been two days without food, she truly regretted her "gluttony." She listened to the squirrels on the roof scurrying about. She walked over to the far wall that was illuminated by the light streak. Using the screw, she drew a diagonal line through the four vertical lines she had already scratched there. *Day five. What's that sound? A car or a truck?* She walked to the door and put her ear to the opening. *No, it's smaller. Maybe a dirt bike or an ATV?* It became louder and then she heard it stop. She jumped up and banged on the walls as hard and loud as she could. "Help! Help! Help!"

She stopped banging and listened. There were

footsteps. *Oh please, God, let them save me.* She banged on the walls and kicked and screamed.

No response.

Oh shit. It wasn't her saviour outside; it was her captor. Anyone else would've called back to her. She sighed.

She heard a scrape of metal on metal. *That's the creaking ladder.* The footsteps were on the roof now and heading towards the hatch, though it didn't open yet.

The spotlight in the corner came on.

"Go to the light," the distorted voice commanded from the roof speaker.

She obeyed.

The hatch opened and the chain came down with a hook. It hooked the handle on the plastic container for her bodily functions and pulled it up through the opening. The hatch closed.

"Stay in the circle of light," the voice reminded her. She stood frozen with fear.

She heard the footsteps moving on the roof and down the ladder. She heard the splash of the contents being emptied. The footsteps returned. The hatch opened again, and slowly another two crates of bottled water, a shoebox, and the empty plastic container were lowered mechanically. The hatch closed. The footsteps went down the ladder again.

She stayed in the circle, but now she yelled and banged on the wall.

"Please, please, please. I have been good. Please

let me go. Don't leave. Please don't leave. Please. I'll do anything. I don't know what to do. Please *let me go*!"

She shook as the tears poured from her eyes and the blood oozed from her hands. "You promised! You said ask and you shall receive! I am asking! I am begging you! Please...."

The light turned off.

She heard the engine start up and spin away in a roar.

The voice came on again, repeating the same mantra: "You asked and you shall receive.

"Drink the water.

"Cherish the food.

"Use the body function container.

"It's that simple."

She walked to the shoebox. The contents were about the same as three days before: three small bags of trail mix nuts and three bananas. In addition to that, there was a carton of milk and a small bag of raisins.

"Bonus." She smirked. *I need to ration it this time. Who knows when he'll be back?*

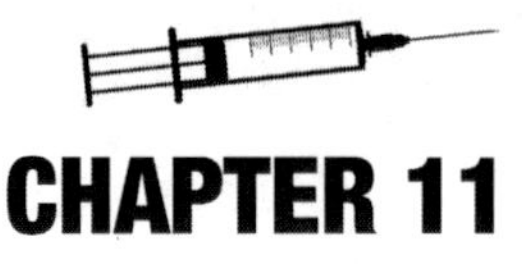

CHAPTER 11

1994: PETRIFIED

From afar, a familiar beep entered into my consciousness. *What is that?*

It hit me.

Fuck, fuck, fuck! It's my bloody pager. I bolted upright in bed, where I had crashed face down. I was still in my work clothes. My stethoscope had left a deep groove on my forehead where I had fallen asleep on it. Disoriented, I scanned the room for the beeping. The pager was still on the belt of my pants lying on the floor. I must've dropped them and fallen asleep in my shirt. It was my third month of residency, and I felt as if I hadn't had one proper night's sleep the whole time. Fatigue oozed from my pores. I felt nauseous all the time, and everything ached. My eyes had dark rings around them and my cheekbones showed.

I washed my face and saw my gaunt expression in the mirror.

Shit, I need to eat better.

The pager went off again.

"Okay, okay." I called in. It was the emergency department.

"Are you the obs and gyne resident on call?" she asked.

"No ... um ... yes. What date is it?" I had to work it out. I had been on call the day before yesterday and I'd assisted yesterday as second on call ... *shit, shit. It is me again.* "Yes, I am on call. What's the problem?"

"We have a sixteen-year-old septic abortion here, Doc. Will you come and see her?"

"Sure."

"Doc?"

"Ja?"

"Just a heads up. Don't take your time. She looks pretty bad."

I was going to shower first, but instead I grabbed a coffee and drove to the hospital.

The nursing union was on strike again. A picket fence of dancing strikers surrounded the hospital. I drove past them all and some of them pushed up against my car. The week before, a baby had died at our neighbouring hospital because the neonatal nurses left the kid unattended and the picket fence would not allow the mother in to pick up her baby. *Fuck the picket fence. No one should get something for doing nothing.* What was the quote? "You don't always get what you work for, but you always work for what you get."

I parked and ran around the back entrance to emergency, trying to avoid the line of patients lying on gurneys outside the department, waiting for their chance to be seen inside. As I entered, one of the emergency nurses sat on the stairs crying.

"What's going on, Ellen?"

"They shook the matches at me when I came in to work today."

"Shook the matches?"

"That's how they say they are going to burn your house down."

"Are you serious?"

"Maybe they just wanna scare me, Doc. I don't know, but I know I'm scared. It's not right. These people are dangerous. I have to go home." I left her crying there on the back staircase. I couldn't fix it anyway.

The sixteen-year-old looked terrible.

"What happened here?" I asked.

She cried and shook her head. Abortion was illegal so she'd had a backstreet abortion in the township. Coat hanger abortions, the nurses called them. The patient wouldn't give me any details, from fear of prosecution. One of the emergency nurses knew her and gave me the information.

The girl was pale and sweaty. Obviously she was having a fever with chills and shivers. Her blood pressure was low and her pulse fast and thready. She was in septic shock.

I felt her abdomen, and it felt like a twelve-week-old pregnancy since the top of uterus seemed to be below the pelvic rim. I looked at my watch. It was 7:04.

Ultrasound wouldn't come in until 9:00. She was too sick to wait. I called the specialist consultant. He would be consulting in his private rooms this morning.

I explained the situation.

"OK, so take her in and do the D&C."

"This one looks a bit complicated. I might perforate the uterus...."

"Sure, we all might perforate the uterus. Come on, if you are worried, do a chest x-ray afterwards, for heaven's sake. If she has free air, then you call me." Free air on an upright chest x-ray would indicate a uterus perforation caused by the procedure—in other words, caused by me.

I booked her for 'the theatre' and was relieved to see that the anaesthetist was Dr. Michael Clarke, busy with his anaesthetic rotation of the residency.

At least my friend would be in the room with me. I called to give him a heads-up.

"Michael, this girl is sick. I have two large lines running and a unit of O-negative blood is coming. She has been cross-matched for six units of blood. Antibiotics are in, but that septic focus needs to come out."

Michael quickly zipped her into the operating room. He appeared to be in his element. He gave brisk, precise orders to the nurse assisting him.

He pulled his mask down and leaned closer to the patient's scared face. He gave her a calm, confident smile and spoke with assurance and no sense of urgency.

"Hi, Thandi. I am Dr. Michael Clarke. I am going to help you sleep, and I will wake you up. I promise you will not feel any pain. Dr. Benáde over there is going make you all better. It is all going to be okay. Do you understand? Uyaqonda?"

The whites of her eyes were clearly visible as fear retracted her eyelids. She nervously nodded her head but she held Michael's gaze. Their eyes were locked for a few seconds. Michael's smile warmed up even more, and he placed his hand on her exposed shoulder. As the fear disappeared, it released her eyelids and a calm washed over her face. The drugs kicked in and her eyelid became very heavy.

"That's what I like to see," he whispered and replaced his mask. He returned to the top end of the bed by the anaesthetic machine and turned the volume of the monitors back on. Alarms started beeping. Her pulse was running fast and her blood pressure was still on the low side. Michael intubated her quickly and looked up.

"All yours, Peter."

I started the D&C to evacuate the uterus. After the first few scrapes, I struck trouble.

"Shit!"

Michael and the nurse looked at me abruptly.

"It's not supposed to be that big. Let me feel that uterus again." I handed the retractors to the nurse and repeated the internal examination.

"Michael, it is way bigger than twelve weeks. I must have misjudged its size as all the amniotic fluid had been drained in the abortion attempt." I turned to the nurse. "This is going to be hard, Julie. I need that," I pointed to the instruments used more for dismantling than for curettage. The object of the procedure changed: I now had to dismantle and remove, instead of just removing. The theatre nurse got pale, sat down on her haunches, and hung her head down, but she was still able to hand me the required instruments. I felt cold shivers run up my spine, a warm flush in my ears, and a mantra in my head: *Stay focused, don't faint, stay focused, you're okay.* As I removed the final, largest piece of fetal product with a 'pop,' a torrent of blood as thick as my arm gushed from the girl, like an open fire hydrant.

"*Fuck!*" My jaw dropped as a freezing chill ran up my spine.

I looked at my nurse in panic. She had her hands on the instrument tray but her head was still hanging between her knees; she was trying not to pass out. She was no help to me now.

Icy cold sweat ran down my armpits and goose bumps raised every hair on my arms.

I looked up and whimpered at my friend.

"Michael—this is bad. She's gonna die. It's just gushing, Michael. *It's gushing!*"

I froze. I swore I could feel Grim Reaper enter the room and look over my shoulder with his icy breath on my neck.

I could not move.

My focus went from the patient to Michael's green

eyes at the top end of the bed. My whole essence screamed: *Get ... me ... out ... of ... here ... now.*

"Peter!" Michael leaned right over the sheet barrier that separated the patient's surgical area from the anaesthetic side. "Peter. Look at my eyes and listen. You are petrified."

He let the words sink in. My brain spun, connecting the dots. *What the hell is he saying?* My mental thesaurus kicked in: *petrified, terrified, unable to move, turned to stony substance.*

Michael did not break eye contact. An eerie, tangible connection kept our eyes linked. The emerald green swallowed me. After what felt like an eternity, he calmly said, "Now listen to me. It is what it is, Peter." He paused. "What will be will be."

I took a slow breath in and held it. Slowly, I let it out. An ocean of calm washed over me. For a moment I was transported in time: I was on the beach at Blouberg. I could hear the sound of a huge wave smashing onto the rocks. Then the moment of silence before the slow, bubbling retreat of the water over the rocks, pebbles, and sand. It felt so real that I could taste the sea salt and feel the clammy, sticky sea air on my skin.

Complete calm descended upon me.

Michael leaned even closer to my face and ordered, "Conquer the fear."

I snapped back to reality and feverishly got in there to stop the bleeding.

Ten minutes later I looked up again. Empty units

of blood hung everywhere. Michael still held a unit of blood in his hands as he squeezed it to get it into her more quickly. I noticed more nurses in the room with pumps running everywhere. I heard Michael talking to intensive care. "Yeah, she is in bad shape. Pressors are running, CVP's up, I just pushed in the eighth unit. Yes, she's had FFPs. Pressure 110 over 70—pulse 100. Ja, Donald, she lost a lot, and with the sepsis on top." Michael nodded. "We'll see, we'll see. Peter did great. Now it's up to you guys upstairs."

I looked over my shoulder to where I'd felt Grim Reaper standing before. There was nothing. *Michael must've repelled him.* It was the first time I'd physically felt Grim Reaper in the room with me.

While having our customary whiskey nightcap that night, Michael became very philosophical. He lifted his glass to make a toast in a dramatic staccato voice. "Petrus: from the Greek word for *rock*. Stone. Turning to stone. Petrrrus became petrrrified." He rolled the 'r's like a drum. He held his glass out and touched mine with the lightest *ching*. "*But* ... you conquered fear. You broke through its grip. You were rock solid, Peter. Petrus! Rock solid."

He paused. "Actually, our friendship experienced petrification today." He played with the words.

"Thanks, Michael. You pulled me through. I'm glad I didn't faint! It sure was a bloody mess."

"There will be blood ... and we're blood brothers. Cheers!" Michael toasted.

Grim Reaper took Thandi thirty-six hours later.

Thereafter I became aware of the cold chill of the Reaper's presence on many occasions. Sometimes he would come right up behind me, and I'd feel his frosty breath on my warm ear as he whispered, "This one is mine."

I could sense the smirk on his face, mocking my best efforts. I knew I'd be fighting him for the rest of my life.

He drew a line in the sand.

Challenge accepted, asshole.

CHAPTER 12

1994: CATWOMAN

"Die kat kom weer!" she yelled as I opened the door. *The cat returns.*

Sandra flung her arms around my neck and gave me a passionate kiss and hug. She glided into our apartment. "Who is where?"

I gave her the quick tour of our two-bedroom flat. It had a central living space with an open-plan kitchen, living room, and balcony. The bedrooms, with en suite bathrooms, were opposite each other, both leading into the central living space. As one entered the apartment, one could appreciate the grand view of the Port Elizabeth King's Beach.

"Michael's room is on that side and mine is over here to the left," I said. "We do have a nice—" She flung her backpack onto my bed. I paused.

She looked at me. "You were saying...?"

I carefully ventured. I didn't want to spoil it, but I could not risk her leading me on only to let me go again. I had reached a point where I could live without her, and it had taken a long time to get there. I called it as I saw it.

"I wanted to say 'pull-out couch,' but it seems we're doing something different now?" I gestured at her bag. "That's my bed."

"I know, Peter. That's your bed. I think you can handle it now. Am I right?"

"Deep down, I am still the same guy."

"I bargained on that." She opened her hand to show me the pebble. It was polished and shiny. "Persistence and time."

She walked straight up to me and took the front lapels of my shirt in her sleek hands. She pulled me closer, looking straight at my chest. Then she looked up. Those crystal blue eyes shattered all resistance. She was calm and more intense than before.

"You offered me the pebble before. May I have it now?" she said.

Absolutely irresistible. I never stood a chance. She came, she saw, she conquered. Resistance was futile.

"Of course. It has always been yours." I smiled, and she hugged me tightly as she placed her head on my chest. Her intoxicating scent drifted up from her hair and filled me with desire. We stood in our embrace for a few seconds, as if contemplating the impact of the choice we had just made.

I snapped out of the spell. "Sorry, I got side-tracked. We have a great bottle of white wine in the fridge. Would you like a glass?"

"Of course! Always."

As she flopped onto the couch, she asked how I had been. We talked and talked and talked. My emotions surprised me. The obsessive, needy, self-centred thoughts were gone. I was truly interested in her journeys and her travels; through Greece and Europe she had gone. I mentioned Michael was on call and would be in later, and she just remarked that she'd "see him whenever." We talked about my residency experiences and life as a brand-new doctor. At some point she stopped me and said, "You've become a man, Peter!"

I felt like *the* man.

We talked into the night. At some point she touched on the postcard she sent from Odd Fellows restaurant.

"You know, those boys were so much fun. They could not believe you and Michael were not gay. When they saw pictures of you two, they said you were too beautiful to be straight." I laughed. "You would've loved it over there. And speaking of the devil, how are things between you and Michael?"

"Very good. Extraordinary actually. It appears current society expects men to have only superficial, farting-around-talking-sport-all-day relationships. Our friendship has a different dimension. The moment that happens between men, it somehow creates some suspicion. But you have been part of it in the past, Sandra. It's special and probably quite unique, I guess."

She smiled knowingly and nodded. “True friends are hard to find.”

We toasted, and I got up to open the next bottle of wine.

When I sat down, Sandra showed me her new tattoos. She had two. On her left ankle was the silhouette of a cat. It consisted of a central thick, sleek ‘S’ transformed into the silhouette of a cat. The top of the S formed one ear, then smoothed over into the back of the cat’s head and neck, and then crossed over to form the cat’s chest with the belly of the S. Another line formed the other ear and face. With a dash of whiskers, it formed a streamlined, minimalist cat silhouette. I didn’t like tattoos, but this was elegant and cool and suited her ankle fine.

When she saw I liked it, she jumped up and turned around. She pulled her pants down to expose her sexy lower back. Two sensual cat eyes looked back at me. These eyes had a more tribal appearance. Ethnic patterns surrounded the large eyes and the vertical slits of the pupils gave them an aggressive appearance. These were the eyes of a big cat, a tiger.

“Now I can always keep an eye on you!”

Michael walked in around midnight. He smiled and hugged Sandra for a long time. With his exceptional ability to assess a situation, he quickly cast his eyes towards my bedroom. Michael obviously saw the backpack on my bed and smiled at Sandra. He appeared fine with it all.

“I am still fun, you know,” Michael teased. “But I

see you've moved on, Catz. You said you would. Let's make a toast."

I poured him a drink.

"To life. Welcome back, Catz."

"Die kat kom weer!" I toasted.

My relationship with Sandra intensified, but Michael was still a part of it. I expressed to Sandra how much Michael had meant to me during the past year and told her about our 'blood brothers' case. Sandra looked at me. "You say it as if he gets nothing in return."

"Well, he doesn't really need me."

"Peter, I can't believe you haven't picked up on it yet. You are completely wrong; he depends on you. You're his anchor." I was confused, and she must've seen it on my face. "Let me explain it this way. You are serious, Peter. We all know that and joke about it, but it's a fact. You have true compassion; you are filled with emotion. Yes, you can get too serious and you can wallow in self-loathing, but you are truly human. Michael doesn't always feel in touch with his humanity. He sometimes feels empty, dead inside. On his own, he feels detached. I think he is so fearless because at times he doesn't even feel like a human being. He needs you; you're his connection with humanity. You are his 'solid guy.' His rock. A kite is unable to fly without someone holding on to the string. You ground him. Because of *you*, Michael can fly."

If you stand too close, you can never see what it is.

Sandra had stepped away.

She saw.

CHAPTER 13

1994: ECSTASY

"Are you okay with this?" I asked him.

"With what?"

"Me and Sandra. It's been a few months. You've kept quiet. I know you two were close before. I just wanted to make sure. We are okay?"

Michael looked at me and smiled. "You guys are great together. Just remember what Mae West said: 'Anything worth doing is worth doing slowly.'"

"Mae West also said, 'I never said it would be easy, I only said it would be worth it.'"

"Let's drink to that!"

He toasted my glass.

After taking a sip, he said, "Enough serious talk. Halloween! The costumes I ordered arrived yesterday. They look spectacular. I got the tickets for the Superheroes party at Seaside's Club. We're all set. Our ride picks us up at seven."

"You have a date?"

"Who needs a date if you're Batman?" he laughed.

The party was an absolute blast. South Africa wasn't into the Halloween culture like the Americans, but we loved a costume party. Of course I was Robin, but I was absolutely outdone by the tight-fitting cat suit that Sandra slipped into. The nightclub was packed to the rafters and we danced into the night. It didn't take long for Batman to hook up with a stunning Superwoman.

"Sofia!" she yelled into my ear while she was dancing with Michael. The thumping beat made it impossible to have any further conversation. Her body talked very loudly, though. She danced with voluptuous hips and breasts. Lust and sex appeal surrounded her. In the early morning hours, the music died down, but a special energy was still present between the four of us. The club owner dropped us off at our place.

We noisily stumbled into the elevator up to the apartment.

In the elevator, Sofia caressed Sandra's hair in her hand and spoke with a strong, passionate, and loud South American accent. "I love your hair. It's so soft!"

"Shh, shhh," I said. "Guys, it's two in the morning."

Sofia waved at me with her wrist. "Oh, Peet-ah, you only live once. Don't worry sooo much."

Michael had the keys to the apartment and led the way. While he unlocked the door with one hand, Sofia held on to the other. I had my arm around Sandra's shoulders as we approached the door. At the door, I guided Sandra forward, but kept my hands on her hips.

It was the smallest gesture that triggered it all. Sofia, upon entering the apartment, turned and reached for Sandra's cheek with her free hand. Their eyes met. Sandra's slight lean into Sofia's hand signalled it was okay. There we were, the four of us standing in the entrance of our apartment, Michael holding onto Sofia's one hand, Sofia's other hand caressing Sandra's cheek and sliding into her hair, and me, stunned, with my hands still on Sandra's hips. I looked over our female partners into Michael's eyes. They were electric with excitement. Michael and I had often come home with two girls by our side, but this had never happened.

Time felt suspended.

Sofia leaned in and gave Sandra a slow, passionate kiss. She pulled Sandra in closer, and the arousal level broke all thresholds. Sofia looked from Sandra to Michael, and placed Michael's hand into Sandra's. Sofia looked towards me and winked with a smile as if to say, "Don't worry, everybody's going to have fun." She then slowly unzipped Sandra's cat suit, which Sandra wore better than Michelle Pfeiffer, and her head slid down to Sandra's breasts and then lower. Sandra tilted her neck back as she felt the pleasure. Sandra's hand glided into Michael's hair and she drew him into a passionate kiss. As this happened I realized Sofia had switched her attentions to my groin.

The world turned into an ocean of tactile, orgasmic sensations and smells.

Magnificent. Out of this world.

The night became an abstract painting hanging in the gallery of my mind: a work of art created by four young bodies. White. Bronze. Dark. Sensual curves. Fragrant smells. Smooth textures. Caring touches. Aromatic tastes. Whispers. Moans. Motion. Sweat. Tremors. Silence.

Slow breath.

Light touch.

Knowing smiles.

The unknown explored. I felt ripped from reality into a world of freedom. No rules, only my senses and pleasures. A sharing of my all with three others, and a breaking free from all the rules, constraints, and limitations I had been struggling with my whole life. I felt truly free to live and experience everything in the moment. No judgments or looming consequences to spoil the pleasure.

One word: ecstasy.

It was an extraordinary experience, but very out of character for me.

By morning we were skinny dipping at King's Beach while the sun struck pink on the horizon.

We never saw Sofia again. She was an exchange student from Columbia and she returned home.

Right after the ecstatic night, we were all a little dazed. I walked onto the balcony to sit in the sun and look at the ocean. "What a night that was!"

Sandra was eating a mango. She was eating it off the skin, and thick, yellow juice was running down her hands onto her elbows. The stickiness of it did not seem to bother her at all as she focused on its sweetness.

She lifted her eyebrows in acknowledgement and mumbled, "Yum. This is *so* good."

"I am still having flashbacks of pure joy. It was surreal. I have never experienced anything like that!"

She smiled and squinted cunningly. "I bet you didn't. A little ways removed from the rules of the Benáde household, I'd think."

"For sure. My dad's only sex advice was: *Hou jou ding uit gate uit, dan bly jou gat uit dinge uit!*"

"Peter, I grew up in Natal! Translate, please."

"Sorry! The direct translation is something like: Keep your thing out of holes and your (ass) hole will stay out of 'things,' or trouble. That was my Sex Education 101—plus the lesson that I had to marry a girl before I could ever have sex with her. Yes, that is a world away from last night."

I took a sip from my beer as Sandra sucked the mango pip.

"Some scenes will be imprinted in my brain forever," I said with a smile. "The closeness between us all. There was that one moment there between you and Michael. It was beautiful but weird ... different. Maybe it was my imagination ... it was all a bit of a blur with all the hormones and alcohol."

Sandra put down the mango pip. She smiled, but slowly shook her head from side to side and looked at me knowingly. "I should've known. You are the worst, Peter. It was a perfectly unique night. Sofia made it work for us, but unfortunately I think we have to let it go now. You think you want something, but you don't realize that you are actually unable to handle it. It is like the moth and the flame for you. It'll consume you. No matter how much you enjoyed that in the moment, it is not in your nature to be so light about something that is so serious for you."

"No, no. I was just wondering," I protested, trying to sound very casual.

"Let's be honest, love. We both know you struggle with sharing certain things. It's just the way you are. It's probably the reason I love you so much. It's what makes you the stable, dependable, and grounded guy I love."

She got up and washed her hands. She walked up to me, put my face in her hands, and kissed me lightly on the lips while she stroked my cheek, gentle as can be.

We would never have a night of such 'ecstasy' again.

We got married on the seventh of January, 1995, on a bed of pebbles by the ocean.

Our beautiful daughter, Esmé—Esmeralda was her full name—was born on the twenty-second of July, 1995. She was another one of life's unexpected curve balls.

I continued to work at the hospital in Port Elizabeth, but the working conditions got worse over the next two years. Patient loads increased and funding decreased. Everything appeared to be coming apart at the seams.

Esmé was about to turn two when I opened the newspaper one day to find the straw that broke the camel's back.

There was an article on the "brain drain from South Africa." It was a report on the large number of professionals leaving South Africa for Australia, England, and Canada, and it discussed the possible reasons for this phenomenon. "Was it the uncertain future, the violence, or was it rather political motivations?" The comment from the health minister on the topic was, "Let them leave. Africa is for Africans."

I flipped. I closed the paper in anger, only to see in the corner of the front page, "Sangoma tells HIV victim to rape white girl for cure. Story on page 5." I sat back and heard Esmé cry indoors.

Sandra, Esmé, and I flew to Canada via London. On the same flight were twelve doctors from my graduating class.

I only cared for one: Michael.

CHAPTER 14

DAY 14

"I am never getting out of here," she mumbled.

What a shit place to die. I know I am dying. I don't even get hungry anymore. It's like a part of me now. I am woozy getting up. That can't be good. I am weak. My mouth's dry, but I drink the water. I am shrinking away.

She walked up to her scratch calendar and counted the days. *It was cold last night....* Fourteen days. It must be the end of September now.

The spotlight came on.

"Go to the light."

She knew the drill.

After the water and shoebox had been lowered, the hatch did not close as it usually did. There was more stuff being thrown down.

A rolled up blanket.

Nice.

A puffy sleeping bag.

Very nice.

A pillow.

Awesome.

A large, thick winter coat.

I must've been really good.

Winter mitts and a pair of warm, fuzzy looking winter boots fell through the opening to the floor last. The hatch slammed shut.

"Thanks!" She yelled at the roof.

Oh shit. How long can I hold on?

Suddenly the voice announced: "Here is the key to your freedom."

She listened to every word as it was explained.

She slumped down to the ground in despair as the impossibility of it dawned upon her and she started to cry.

Jesus, I am going to fucking die in here.

CHAPTER 15

1998: THE MOON

On the thirty-first of January, 1998, we landed in Kamloops, British Columbia, Canada. It was a freezing day, and we huddled up in thick layers of clothing, feeling the extreme cold pinch every piece of exposed skin. Driving to the hotel in whiteout conditions, we gazed out the windows in terror.

Holy mackerel. I can't believe people live here. Taking off in plus thirty-five degree weather in Cape Town, we landed in minus twenty-five degree conditions in Kamloops. *Maybe we should take the next plane out of here.*

I flicked on the weather channel in the hotel room.

"Well, it could be worse! It's minus forty in Saskatoon. There are a couple of my classmates going there." I tried to lighten the mood.

Sandra was not impressed. "It's the bloody moon. Cold white and a hell of a way back home. I bet it takes astronauts less time to get home from the moon than what we've just done." She turned to Esmé. "And how am I supposed to get these hands into mittens? You're gonna freeze, my little kitten!"

There was a bang on our door. I opened it for Michael.

"The city of Gotham is under siege from Mr. Freeze!" Michael was in great spirits for some reason. He was obviously referring to the previous year's *Batman and Robin*, featuring Arnold Schwarzenegger as Mr. Freeze. Come to think of it, George Clooney played Batman, and Michael was a dead ringer for him, which I found a bit freaky.

"Are you guys going down for dinner? I hear they have a great Angus steak."

Sandra turned to him. "You're chirpy."

He shrugged. "Hey, it is what it is. I'm buying a snowboard tomorrow. I hear Sun Peaks is a spectacular ski resort—and look at all the white powder!" He waved towards the window.

"Peter, are you coming to the hospital with me tomorrow? I want to have a look at their brand-new emergency room."

"Yes, I will, and then Sandra and I meet with the realtor at twelve to look at houses."

"Are you guys buying or renting a place?"

"I want to rent first, but on the other hand, I don't really want to move around. If we find a place we like, we might actually buy and get properly settled in."

I looked over at Sandra.

Sandra pulled a face of discontentment. "Did you know they construct houses with wood here?"

She had grown up in an expensive, architecturally designed house built from brick, like most high-end properties in South Africa. “It does not make sense to me. I can’t even tell Esmé the fairy tale of the three piggies anymore, because the piggies flee to a brick house that the wolf could not blow down!”

Obviously she was grumpy, moody, and jet-lagged out of her skull.

To love something is not an emotion; it’s a commitment. The commitment had been made. She only needed time.

CHAPTER 16

1998: LIGHTS AND SIRENS... BRING IT ON!

The bat phone—as it was called in the emergency room—went off, and Caroline, the charge nurse, answered. "Go ahead."

She repeated the message as the ambulance attendant talked, to keep us in the loop.

"Nineteen-year-old male."

"Stabbed chest on Seymour Street."

"CPR in process."

"ETA two minutes."

Michael lived for this stuff. I looked at the clock. At least it wasn't shift change. The ambulance crew seemed skilled. Caroline always ran a tight ship, and Michael was the attending emergency physician. This boy was lucky—he might have a chance.

Michael snapped out the orders. To the receptionist: "Overhead announcement: Trauma Level One." To Caroline: "Call OR stat for rib spreaders. I will grab the thoracotomy pack." He grabbed the phone in his pocket and dialled. "Blood bank? Great. Dr.

Michael Clarke in ER. We need six units O negative or positive *stat*." He paused to let it sink in. "Are we clear that I said *stat*? Okay, just checking." He smiled. Into the trauma room: "Peter, you run the head. Tube when you can. RT, you assist him. I will run the left chest wall. Peter, when the tube is in, do the other side. Let's hope he has lines. If not, Julie, get the IO's ready."

He stopped and looked at the team. "This is what we do, people. This is what we do! Everyone gloved? Everyone's got glasses and scrubs?"

We stood and waited with nervous anticipation, everyone's hands in front of them with interlocking fingers to keep the gloves clean. Silence and calm descended, and the suction catheter's *whoosh* was the only white noise. Armed and ready.

They rolled in and spun the story as the well-oiled and prepped machine of trauma bay jumped into action at the same time. It was like a wheel change at a Formula One race. When he hit the bed, everyone knew what to do. Thoracotomies are not commonly done in Canada, but where we came from it was different. Been there. Done that. Got the fucking T-shirt: "This is a stabbed heart."

It is a high-risk procedure for select patients, and you really need to know what to do, but more importantly you need the guts to put a scalpel to a man's chest and zip it open from side to side. That was what distinguished Michael from many others. There was no hesitation. He looked at it. Took the blade and opened that boy up in a second. He went straight in and plugged the hole in the heart with his left index. He held the boy's heart in his right hand and pumped it.

"Foley catheter!" he ordered.

He stuck it in to plug the hole and removed his finger. He continued the cardiac massage with his right hand. We battled hard, and somehow that boy made it to the OR where the damage could be fixed. A life was saved.

A legend was born.

After the incident, Caroline walked over to Michael, and I heard her whisper to him, "Michael, that was amazing. It needed to be done and you did it. Done." She gave him a deep nod of respect. She was clearly impressed, and with her vote of confidence, the nursing staff would never challenge his competency again.

Michael's professional relationships with other disciplines quickly established him as a force to be reckoned with. Emergency medicine was a relatively new specialty, and thus some old school specialists did not truly recognize it yet. They would treat the ER doctors like their servants rather than their peers. Michael nipped this in the bud pretty quickly.

I walked into the doctor's room one night, getting ready for the night shift. Michael had taken a phone call to this room, for some privacy from the gossiping ears of the nursing staff. He was discussing a urological emergency case with the urologist on call. Dr. Carl Du Pont was a fifty-seven-year-old urologist, renowned for being a grumpy French man. The case they were discussing involved a patient with torsion of the testes; when the testicle is twisted around its own blood supply, it creates extreme pain and can result in the rapid loss of that essential organ. Du Pont was grilling Michael for more details about the case in an attempt to avoid coming to the hospital in the middle of the night.

Michael realized what was going on and said, "Wow, Carl, sorry to interrupt you, but which part of 'I suspect this patient has torsion of the testes' is confusing to you?" An angry voice thundered on the other side of the line. Michael didn't waver and became very calm. "No, no, no. Let me explain to *you* what my expectations are from this point on. I want you to see this patient immediately. I am noting the current time of 11:13 right here on the chart. And *no*, I am not phoning you back with an ultrasound report, as I expect you to be here when it is available. I will ask radiology to call the ultrasound technician in, and you can get the results directly from them after you have seen this patient. I hope I have been clear. Are we clear?"

I could hear a 'Who the hell do you think—' echo down the line as Michael slowly put the phone back on the receiver.

He smiled. "Some assholes need to be made aware of their own responsibilities, and you know I won't be bullied. Anyway, once he sees the torsion, he'll shut up. He'll realize I just saved his irritating

French butt from litigation by dragging him in here."

Right he was, and the urologist basked in the glory from the appreciative patient and nurses, who all commented on his commitment to see the patient after hours. Michael made no public comment, and Du Pont never questioned any of his calls again.

The same happened with a patient with a possible ectopic pregnancy, where the pregnancy is abnormally implanted outside the uterus. It can be life threatening. The earlier the diagnosis is made, the better, but sometimes in the early stages it is very difficult to distinguish this serious condition from a less life-threatening one, like a miscarriage.

Michael felt his patient had an ectopic pregnancy, but when he called the gynaecologist, Dr. Angela Baker, he got the run-around.

I remembered his words and loved them. "No, you misunderstood me, Angela. The Quantitative B HCG is not going to give us the answer. She has a clinical ectopic. You need to see her." I could hear her raising her voice on the other end of the line. "It is not that I don't trust your opinion, Angela. I just feel you can't actually *have* a clinical opinion until you physically put your lovely hands on her belly." He allowed his words to sink in. "I'd love to hear your opinion at that time, but till then, I recommend you listen to me." There was silence on the other end of the line. "So when can we expect to see you?" I only partially recognized her voice over the phone. Michael nodded. "Yes, Angela, that's correct. It *is* one in the morning. Great. I think it's a good call.... Don't worry about that. I can warn the OR for you. See you in fifteen, then?" When he had replaced the receiver, he said, "She'll love me for it. She just doesn't know it yet."

Of course, he was right again. The next morning, I overheard Angela talking to a colleague in the doctor's lounge. "I am so glad I took that girl to the OR, you know. She had a belly full of blood and the tube was already tearing by the time we got in there."

Michael kept the specialists honest. He forced them to come in and do what needed to be done, but he let them get the glory and the credit for doing it. All of these episodes of 'encouragement' happened behind closed doors. He never embarrassed any specialist publicly in the department, and maintained respectful professionalism. They quickly returned his respect.

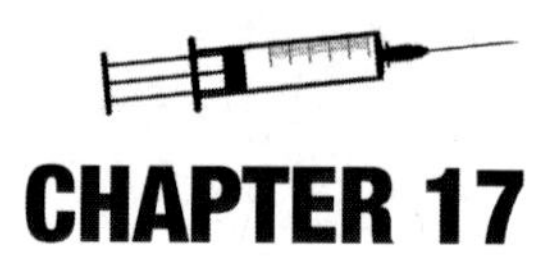

CHAPTER 17

2005: BATMAN BEGINS

Oh man, isn't that the best bloody Batman movie ever?" Michael found it difficult to contain himself as we walked out of the cinema. "Christopher Nolan is a genius. Loved the grit. Loved the reality."

"I thought a purist like you would be upset? It didn't have a comic book feel at all."

"No, but I loved it. It had real-world roots. I read that it is a trilogy of movies. This was spectacular. I can't wait for the other two!"

The movie fired up Michael's Batman fetish again, and whenever we had a few drinks, he dragged out his comic books more regularly. Since we were doing pretty well financially and Michael was a bachelor, he could spend money on all sorts of extravagant things married men never got away with. He started collecting Batman art. I never even knew that existed, but Michael would follow specific editions of comic books or sketches of specific scenes. He would bid and buy these artworks at auctions. He even visited

Heritage Auction House in Dallas, Texas. On his wall he mounted the original 1942 Detective Comics #67, *First Penguin Cover in Pen and Ink*, which depicted Batman and Robin chasing the Penguin riding an ostrich. He never told me what he paid for it, but I saw on the auction records that an anonymous buyer had bought it for $239,000.

He also had a framed cover of the original 1943 Detective Comics #76—*Slay 'em with Flowers*—as part of his enlarging collection. He said it wasn't very valuable, but he loved the cover, which featured the Joker with a large poison syringe about to squirt Batman and Robin. Spending so much money on comic books was strange to me, but somehow Michael felt it was worth it.

He built himself a beautiful house outside town. In the Cherry Creek area, west of town, a small gravel road called Deer Road took you up to his block of land, with its majestic view over Kamloops Lake. The house was invisible from the main road to Savona, and the large, solid, wood front door had the words "The Cave" engraved on it.

On entering the house, it always reminded me of the apartment we shared in Port Elizabeth. It had a surprisingly modern look, with large floor-to-ceiling glass on the cliff side overlooking the lake. There were no curtains or blinds, only expansive views.

The railing on the deck was frameless glass, and walking to the edge gave me vertigo as I looked over the cliff to the lake far below. Downstairs was a study with a bar, a fireplace, and two comfortable reading chairs in the centre of the space. Very minimalist. It had the simplicity of four sides: wine, books, fire, and view. The house faced west and had the best sunset views ever. Many sundowners would be enjoyed there.

Even though the house was stunning, its location out of town caused me to see less of Michael. He began to live a life of greater solitude and eccentricity. His lightness never disappeared, but he became more philosophical, reflective, and detached. His pauses in conversation were just a fraction longer than they used to be. His smiles held a little more cynicism.

It wasn't only Michael that was changing. We all were.

■ ■ ■

Relationships and toxicology have a lot in common.

One: A sufficient amount of almost any medication can make a poison.

Two: If a drug has an effect, it will have side effects.

Three: The body is in balance. Every desired effect will need to be compensated for elsewhere to restore its balance. Thus there is no such thing as a drug with only positive treatment effects and no side effects. Every pill has side effects and will become poison if you overdose.

And in relationships, the attributes that draw people together cause change and eventually can cause them to break up. If you're attracted to your partner because he is so calm and relaxed, he will repel you later for being too laid-back. The exciting risk-taker will lose his wife because eventually she will find him too irresponsible. The cool, intriguing, and mysterious girl later gets accused of being frigid or having an affair.

With us it was no different. I impressed Sandra initially with my stability and my ability to be a dependable provider, but through the years I began to irritate her by working too hard and being too boring on the social scene.

I fell in love with Sandra because she was an elusive and energetic person who added spice to everything. However, it infuriated me when she who would go on expensive shopping sprees or impulsively board a plane with a mere, "See you on Monday, honey!"

We could not see the characteristics we fell in love with anymore; they had been transformed into ones that irritated the hell out of us.

It became a true tidal relationship, an ebb and flow of nasty fights that alternated with make-up sex. We were both in an emotional limbo, riding out the tides, hoping for a better tomorrow. JC Watts said it best: "It doesn't take a lot of strength to hang on; it takes a lot of strength to let go." The co-dependency of living in a foreign country and Esmé, of course, kept us together, but our relationship drifted towards an abyss.

Our fights had little trigger words in them. Words like *always* and *never* were little landmines laid out for the other to step on: "You're always late from work! Can you never be on time for a dinner!" I probably irritated Sandra more by noticing these tripwires and then making it an intellectual game of sidestepping them. She would stir a fight to provoke me into packing my bags and taking the initiative to leave.

I'm no quitter.

Neither of us had the courage to go. In weakness we both stayed, *for better or for worse*, a lion and a lamb clinging to each other in a flooding river.

Sandra enjoyed the comfortable life I provided, but I knew she could fill the obvious voids of our relationship elsewhere. She certainly had opportunities for such extramarital escapades, as I worked long hours—to pay the bills she racked up. My paranoia started to grow and my self-confidence waned. The victories of Grim Reaper enforced this.

Jealousy and paranoia grew in me like a cancer. Pancreatic cancer to be exact. Infamously difficult to detect, the cancer eats your guts as it slowly grows and causes discomfort in the pit of your stomach. You feel uneasy and nauseated for months, and no one can figure out why. When it eventually gets diagnosed, it's usually too late. You turn yellow and get ready to receive your last round of Christmas cards. Insidiously lethal.

■ ■ ■

Michael was the one to break the news to me.

"Hey, Peter—who said 'things are never so bad that they can't be made worse'?

"Isn't it Murphy's law?"

"Sort of, but you're off your game. It's Humphrey Bogart."

I sighed. "So what is it now?"

"I hate to break this to you, but guess who got appointed as the new anaesthetist and intensive care specialist."

"Who?"

"Raise the Dead Halstead."

Fuck. "I hate that arrogant ass. Why the hell would he come here? Isn't he like king of the hill in South Africa, with all his bloody publications and fame? He's the South African guru on aggressive sepsis management, isn't he?"

"That's where the nickname came from."

"Why'd he leave?" I asked.

"Don't really know. He might the king of sepsis, but I think he screwed up somewhere else. Maybe the dean's wife or burnout or something. All I know is it's all very hush-hush. Obviously ICU and anaesthetics are ecstatic to have him. He is an asshole, but he's good at what he does."

"I know, but, 'Of all the gin joints, in all the towns, in all the world'*....*"

Michael just smiled and shook his head. He wrapped his arm around my slumped shoulders and walked me to my car.

"Don't stress. She'll never go for him, Peter. Never."

CHAPTER 18

DAY 30

First light. The squirrel was up already; he was a scurrying reminder every day that winter was coming. She slowly sat up. It had been cold last night, but the sleeping bag kept it cozy. She took a sip of water, walked over to the scratch calendar, and crossed out the sixth stack of five. One month. *Who would've thought I had it in me?* A wry glimpse of a smile appeared in the corner of her mouth.

She shuffled to the container and peed a few drops.

She started her walk round the perimeter of the box and counted the laps. *One. Two. Three. Four. Five.*

She breathed heavily and leaned against the wall to catch her breath. *Six. Seven.*

She fell down on her mat, exhausted and dizzy.

Tomorrow I'll try to get to ten again.

She waited for the daily voice, and soon the speaker crackled to life.

"Strip," it said.

Okay, we're doing this now.

She undressed.

She placed her clothes neatly on her yoga mat.

She shuffled to the corner and waited for the light to come on.

CHAPTER 19

2010: THE DARK KNIGHT

The twenty-fourth of November, 2010. It was a bluebird day at Sun Peaks ski resort. I sat on the Sunnyside ski run, facing south, feeling the sun on my face. A panoramic view lay stretched out in front of me. Ten inches got dumped the night before, but the snow clouds left a bright, sunny day behind. It was absolutely perfect for snowboarding.

I sat in complete silence waiting for Michael. Blue skies. Crystal white snow. Time suspended high on a mountaintop. Tranquillity.

He sent me a text saying he had arrived at Sun Peaks. I told him where to meet me.

Who would have guessed Michael would be dead exactly one year later, to the day?

With a *boom*, a spray of white powder covered me as Michael landed a jump a few yards away. He was laughing. "It's awesome! Pow-pow everywhere!"

He took a quick glance around as if he was trying to figure out what I was looking at. He looked at me. In a raspy voice he guttered, "Why ... so ... serious?" He laughed again. Obviously he was on an endorphin and adrenaline high. He couldn't let any opportunity slip by to mimic Heath Ledger and the legendary Joker from the latest Batman movie, Christopher Nolan's *The Dark Knight.*

"Let's put a smile on that face!"

He turned, and down the slope he went. I followed and tried to keep up. Michael was a very aggressive boarder. He floated through the knee-deep powder, hitting stumps, jumps, and ledges on the way down. I stuck to the middle of the slope and did long, slow carves through the beautiful powder. We drifted to the sides where the powder was still undisturbed. "Virgin powder, woo-hoo!" I heard Michael holler. When I got to the chairlift, he was waiting for me. "How've you been buddy? Haven't seen you for a while!" he said as we got on.

"I've been busy. Work, you know. Yourself?"

"Same old, same old. Same shit, different day. I love my house. I love getting out of town at the end of the day. You should come over after a shift or whenever. Bring Catz, if you want."

"It's been testy between us. I think I'll probably come on my own. What have you been up to? Are you becoming a recluse?"

"I grew tired of the party scene. Being single has its benefits for sure, but I am sick of the introductions and getting to know the person and then the trying to get rid of them. I tell you, these days I'd rather read a good book or board with a buddy. And as for the sex—well, they don't call me *hand*some for no reason," he laughed. "Wasn't it your favourite, Mae West, who said, 'Sex is like bridge: If you don't have a good partner you'd better have a good hand'?"

"Good one, yeah, but come on, Michael. I know you better than that. You can snap your fingers and you'll have a team of girls in your bed."

"Getting them into my bed isn't my problem. It's getting them out that spoils it for me. Many times it's not worth it. I love the chase, but get bored quickly with what I've caught."

"Great problem to have. I am so tired of our battles at home; maybe I should call it quits. We're both going through a transitional phase in life. Maybe we need to acquaint ourselves with the people we're becoming before we can have a real relationship again. I am afraid she might not like the person I am turning into. I'm not even sure that *I* like the person I'm becoming."

"What do you mean?"

"I don't know.... People irritate me all the time. Most people get under my skin. The nurses are on my case, the guys we work with.... Shit, they are so lazy and keep dumping crap on me every shift. The patients are just thankless pricks most days. I feel unsettled inside. Discontented."

Michael allowed those words to hang out there for a while. It felt great to blurt them out. I could feel the anger, frustration, and hatred evaporate as the wind took my words. To rid one's heart of negative emotions, sometimes you just need to say it out loud, to a true friend—someone who knows you well enough to know that you're not truly the ass you sound like.

Halfway up, Michael started to talk. "It's the generation of 'everyone for himself.' They think an emergency department is a McDonald's drive-through, and the longer they wait, the more they think they have earned the right to have more of your time. You know what I mean? The crumpled sheet of paper with the scribbled list of twenty problems, nicely categorized with date and time of occurrences, starting at the fucking turn of the century. 'Doc, you're mine now, you've got to fix all of this.'"

"Yes, isn't it weird? The longer they have had the problem, the more serious they think it is. Meanwhile, if it has been there for more than a few hours it probably isn't an emergency at all. Emergencies are the things that kill you quickly; the rest is supposed to be someone else's problem to fix.

"It's funny when you ask, 'How long have you had the rash?' and they truly think they are going to knock your socks off: 'For years, Doctor!' And all I can think is, 'So what's the freaking emergency then?' But of course you don't say it. You have to smile and say the politically correct thing. 'Oh, that's terrible. Now why did you decide to visit us today at three in the morning? Did it change?' 'Oh no, Doc, I just couldn't stand it anymore.'"

Michael smiled.

"It's frustrating for sure! It's a spoilt and comfortable

society, and we're at their beck and call. And then, like a pubic hair on a toilet seat, eventually you're gonna get pissed off!" He laughed and shrugged.

We reached the top.

"Let's burn it, baby!"

We hopped off and turned right towards the black diamond runs down the Headwalls. At the top of Headwalls, I sat down for a moment to absorb the beauty. Michael didn't slow down; he did a bunny hop over the steep edge and burned it down the slope, carving hard and throwing big plumes of white on each turn. Aggressive. Fearless. On the edge of losing all control.

CHAPTER 20

DECEMBER 31, 2010: NEW YEAR'S EVE

Someone always got the short straw. At the end of 2010, it was my turn. Our graveyard night shifts started at eleven. I took a nap before the shift and got up at ten. I had a coffee, snuck into Esmé's room, and kissed her on the forehead. Although it was New Year's Eve, my night shift screwed up the possibility of a party, and thus Sandra went to bed early when I went for my pre-shift nap. With her asleep, I dressed in my scrubs quietly. I made myself a sandwich for the three a.m. hunger and snuck down to the garage. I quietly rolled my car out and drove to the hospital. My eyes were still burning with sleep, and I had a bit of a chill in my back. As I approached the last traffic light before the hospital, a familiar thought hit me: *Fuck, I hate graveyard shifts.*

I looked up at the high-rise vertical lines of the hospital and the helipad lights on top of the roof as they shone into the night. The fog was rolling in. It looked eerie, like a charcoal sketch of Gotham City.

I could see an ambulance in my rear-view mirror, racing with lights and sirens towards the hospital. Abiding by the traffic rule in British Columbia, I slowed down and pulled over to let the ambulance scoot by. *What's the rush, buddy? Who do you think is going to fix the patient inside your ambulance? Now I have to pull over for you? Stupid....*

I drove to the parking area, turned my vehicle off, and sat there for a few seconds staring at the side door entrance. I could hear my thoughts as if clearly spoken: *What am I doing? Can't I just walk away? Nothing can force me to get out of this car. No one can compel me to walk inside. Maybe I could just drive away. Maybe I can go to a warm spot in the sun. Just drive, just leave, just get out of here. Why don't I?*

"Aggghh ... fuck it. Stop whining, Peter," I said out loud.

I got out. I slowly walked to the entrance door. As my hand touched the door handle, I paused. I put on my smile and walked through.

"Hi, everyone! Happy New Year's, eh! How's the evening been? Do we have beds upstairs?" And so the night began.

At least I was working with a great team of nurses. The charge nurse was Caroline, which meant the ER would run as well as it was able to. She would create that magical thing called 'ER flow' by employing her exceptional organizational skills and experience. Caroline was a force to be reckoned with. She kept doctors on their toes by challenging and guiding them to see patients more efficiently. She pushed the ward staff to take admitted patients out of the ER as quickly as possible, and she got really tough on patients who abused the system or visited the ER unnecessarily. She tried her utmost to make a struggling emergency care system work. Never married, she devoted her life to nursing. Her motto was, "We can't always cure, but we can always care."

And then there was Tracy. She was a newly graduated nurse. She was very green, a bit slow in getting things done and prone to medical errors that at times bordered on negligence, but she was a pure pleasure to look at. At twenty-four, she was gorgeous, with dark eyes and long black hair that she always neatly tied up behind her head. Her athletic body showed even through the terribly fashioned ER scrubs. One could not help but smile when she was working with you. Her appearance alone was of medicinal value for the men in the department.

It didn't take too long for the old familiar names to start arriving. I usually do not recall patients' names. A familiar name is a bad thing; it's a frequent flyer. Usually my frequent flyers, like the homeless alcoholics who'd burned all their bridges at the shelters and social assistance, had insoluble social problems. They had only the hospital left to go to, because we could not turn anyone away. To add insult to injury, many of them also had legitimate medical and addiction problems. They could suck the marrow out of your shift.

Now they were all rolling in, one after the other. The first one was the familiar Mr. David Morin. He was 'found unconscious' on a park bench by a passer-by. That Good Samaritan felt it was his duty to call the police. The police called the ambulance, and thus he was presented to the emergency in a state of extreme intoxication ... again. As usual, the distinct, sweet smell of mouthwash was all over him. He would drink litres of it, as it was much cheaper than normal alcohol. When he sobered up he was usually quite comical, but it only lasted until his withdrawals kicked in. Then he got belligerent, grumpy, and shaky. Eventually, he would leave the department to get a drink.

He originally came from Sandy Bay, Saskatchewan. According to circulating rumours, he was a convicted felon in a case of manslaughter. On a winter's night in northern Saskatchewan, he and his friends were intoxicated and high when David's front door was left unlocked, and his four-year-old niece walked out into the cold and froze to death. He got the blame. I always felt conflicted by these predicaments. Some people are simply born into miserable lives, and in order to survive, they end up doing bad things, intentionally or unintentionally. Who was I to judge? Michael, however, simply hated his guts. "He is a useless parasite. Weeds like him just keep on living, and then the kids die!" Life was black and white to Michael.

David toured around with his travel buddy, Craig Villaincourt. They were both homeless and had succeeded in burning all their bridges with the men's hostels and care facilities in town. Every now and then, a new community social worker would attempt to help them. It would work for a while, and then Craig or David would somehow default by assaulting a fellow patron or staff member, or drinking or smoking in the wrong areas. Sleeping on park benches would trigger well-meaning citizens to 'do the right thing' and dial 911. Thus, Craig and David frequently ended up on our emergency doorstep.

When people fall through the cracks, the emergency room is the final dragnet that catches them all. Again and again and again.

I said hello to David and asked how Craig was. I left him sleeping his rust off for the night on the only bed he knew, an emergency room gurney. Caroline had already placed juice and a sandwich on the table at the end of his bed, to enable him to get discharged in the morning. She had little time for these 'abusers of the system,' but was clever enough to know that the quickest way to free up his bed was to get David sober and give him something to eat.

Then Chad Bishop could be heard presenting himself to the ER. The hollering of F-words was unmistakable. Caroline was covering the triage area. She knew him well and spoke to Chad in a motherly tone. She told him firmly that she would allow him "one chance to sit down and be quiet" and tell her why he needed help, but if she heard one more curse, she was pressing the red button and he'd be gone. She reminded him that the police were busy on New

Year's Eve and might not have a lot of patience for big guys like him abusing the nursing staff at the only ER in town. He shut up and sat down. He was a huge muscular guy. He had no neck, and his arms looked as if they were infused with anabolic steroids. He was more a pill-popper and dealer than an intravenous user—his veins still seemed unscarred and bulging. He struggled with addiction.

Of course his complaint was that "someone had stolen" his narcotic prescription drugs. The 240 tablets dispensed the previous day were all "stolen." *Same old story.*

After she had triaged him, Caroline came over to me. "Chad Bishop is waiting for you. Now don't you get sucked into his nonsense tonight, Peter. When we bring him in, you get him out. I don't want trouble. I will pull up his pharmacy dispensing history. I am sure he sees Halstead for pain management—"

"Halstead is running a pain clinic now?" I interrupted.

"Yes, with some of the other anaesthetists." She appeared irritated that I interrupted her. "Anyway, you got me side-tracked there. As I was saying, get him in and get him out. He mixes with the wrong crowd, and someday soon someone's going fix that problem differently. But tonight he is ours." Typical Caroline: keeping the ER flowing.

By the time I got to see Chad in the minor treatment area, two hours had passed and he was getting riled up again. "Hi, Mr. Bishop, I am Dr. Benáde. How can I help you?"

Chad Bishop was lying on a bed. He wasn't looking at me. He was writhing, moaning, and holding on to his back with one hand and his left leg with the other. He wasn't aware I had actually witnessed him register a few hours earlier, when none of those complaints existed.

"Hi, Doc. My back and leg are killing me. You must refill my prescription."

I felt the flush reach my cheeks, and the hair on the back of my neck stood on end. *There are many things in life that I must do, Chad, but being your drug supplier isn't one. There are truly sick people I need to help. Why do I have to waste my time with this guy?*

I took a slow, deep breath.

Peter, just give him a chance to tell his story. Stay calm. Let's not ruin the shift this early. Smiling friendly, I asked, "What prescription is that?"

"It's on my bloody chart there! My Percs."

"I see on your PharmaNet printout that you filled that narcotic prescription yesterday, so I don't think I can help you with *that* at this time."

"My stuff was stolen, Doc." His moaning reached a crescendo. "Aah! What am I supposed to do now, Doc? I'm in agony!"

"Well, my recommendation is for you to report a theft to the police. As you know, you are only supposed to see Dr. Halstead, your pain specialist, for your chronic pain prescriptions, not the ER. You are double doctoring at the moment."

"So you mean to tell me I have been waiting for four hours for nothing? What kind of doctor are you? I am in pain here!"

"Chad, I can help you with your pain. I can suggest some pain killers or give you an injection to help you till you can see your doctor."

"What will you give me?"

Oh boy, here it starts. "Well, Chad, I was thinking Tylenol."

"I am allergic to that," he snapped at me.

"Okay then, ibuprofen would be an alternative."

"That doesn't work and I have had an ulcer. I already told you only Percs work for me!" He was raising his voice.

This is going nowhere. I have other people to see. Just let it go, Peter. Caroline saw this coming.

"Well, Chad, I am willing to help you but unfortunately not with that prescription, so it does appear we are out of ideas for tonight. Please contact your family physician or pain specialist Dr. Halstead tomorrow."

"Yeah right, you fucking foreign prick! He's away on holiday! Where the fucking hell are you from anyway? Australia? New Zealand?"

"Chad. I have to go now, I'm sorry," I said with the little bit of restraint I had left.

"Don't tell me you're a fucking South African, Doc. No wonder you know nothing, useless piece of shit!"

I turned and asked Tracy to call security. The announcement came overhead.

I walked to the nurse's station, but then, unbeknownst to Chad, I turned around to check how he would be leaving the department. He was furious, mumbling and swearing. When he heard the announcement for security, he jumped off the bed in one quick movement. He quickly leaned over and tied his shoelaces, grabbed his backpack, and walked out of the minor treatment area exit door at a brisk pace, slamming the door on his exit. His disabled leg and back pain was 'miraculously' cured in ten seconds. *And the Oscar goes to....*

The night continued, and I slogged on. One of the other regulars was Mr. Earl Patterson. He was a grumpy old guy. He had emphysema from smoking fifty cigarettes a day while on home oxygen. He knew that he shouldn't be doing both, but no one had been able to stop him smoking, and no one felt it right to suffocate him by taking his oxygen away. If we did, he would only spend more time in hospital.

I walked in and, as was my habit, said, "Hi, I am Dr. Benade, the emergency doctor. I have seen you before, how can I help you tonight, sir?" As I said it, I recalled his pet peeve ... too late.

"I am not your *sir*!"

"Okay, Mr. Patterson, I apologize. I forgot. Is it your lungs again today?"

After Mr. Patterson, Caroline called me over immediately to see Mrs. Catherine Campbell. She had fallen and broken her hip. She was in pain, and Caroline needed my order for morphine. Caroline had it already drawn up in a syringe, just awaiting my order. She explained the side effects of morphine to Mrs. Campbell and said she would give her a small amount first to see how it worked for her. As she was injecting it slowly, Mrs. Campbell took Caroline's arm firmly and looked up into her eyes. "Inject it all."

"I can't do that, Mrs. Campbell. It could stop your breathing."

"I know exactly what it does. I am a retired nurse. Just give it all, please. I don't wanna live without George." She started sobbing. "We were married for fifty-six years. He died three months ago. Please, nurse." She was crying.

Caroline looked into her eyes. "I know, love. It is hard, but you know I can't do that. I will get a few things sorted out and then I'll come and talk to you in a few minutes, okay?" She gave Mrs. Campbell a compassionate smile as she removed her arm from her grip and withdrew the morphine-filled syringe from the intravenous line. "Is the pain at least a bit better now?" Mrs. Campbell nodded as the tears streaked over her cheeks. I would need to get her hip fixed by orthopaedics—and get a psychiatric assessment.

Caroline was something special. During her break, she pulled a chair closer and had her tea with Mrs. Campbell. She listened quietly as Mrs. Campbell spoke about her husband George and the life they had had together. Mrs. Campbell did have a broken hip, and it took quite a bit of convincing to get her to consent to surgery, as she had strong suicidal thoughts and reactive depression. Finally, she consented, but wanted a Do Not Resuscitate order to be in place. "Just in case."

Night became morning.

At 4:45 the familiar nauseating sickness of fatigue and hunger rose in my stomach. Drained and dragging my feet, I slipped away to eat my sandwich and awoke when my phone went off. I had nodded off with a half-eaten sandwich in my hand.

I looked at my watch. 5:00 a.m. *Only two more hours.*

At 6:30 the end was in sight, and I returned to the minor treatment area. That was when I picked up the chart for Amelia Blair.

It was the first time I saw her.

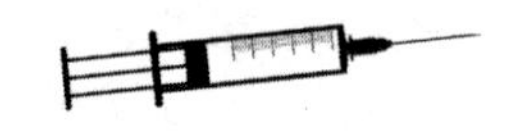

CHAPTER 21

6:30 A.M., JANUARY 1, 2011: AMELIA BLAIR

I slipped through the cubicle curtain to face the expansive white T-shirt that spanned her back. The rolls of fat created the strange illusion that she had two magnificent breasts stuck on the wrong side of her body. She shyly looked over her right shoulder. I looked down at the chart. *Oh boy. Only twenty-six, and she is already this overweight.* She had a friend with her.

"Hi, Doc. This is my friend, Doherty Christy," she said with a friendly smile.

She must've picked up that I was puzzled about the purpose of a friend for the visit, because she immediately said, "Doherty, would you give us a moment?" Doherty slipped out. She was a very large girl herself. I rounded Amelia's bed to face her. Although she was very chubby, she had quite an attractive face. She sat with her feet on the step we provided to enable shorter people to get onto the hospital beds. Her small feet were a few feet apart to allow for the stomach apron of fat to come down between her thighs to the bed level. The large T-shirt was complimented by some loose sweat pants. White socks on her feet; winter boots next to the bed. *Wal-Mart dress code ... ugh. I'm getting just as nasty as Michael. I hope this is quick and easy; I need to get some sleep.*

"Hi, I am Dr. Benáde. How can I help today?"

"I am bit overweight...." She spoke in a high-pitched tone that sounded like a budgie chirp, but she maintained a sweet smile and a shy blush. "Otherwise, I am a 350-pound, healthy girl." She blushed and smiled again.

"Those terms are mutually exclusive, actually," I mumbled as I looked down to write a note on her chart. When I looked up, I could see the hurt on her face. The guilt struck me. *What the hell are you thinking? It's not her fault that you're tired. Get a grip!*

"Sorry, um—" I read her name from the chart, "Amelia. That was really insensitive of me. I apologize; it's been a long night. I am truly sorry. How can I help? What is the reason for you being here?"

"So the reason I'm here.... Yes, I am a very big girl, or the truth, as you can see ... I'm fat. Very fat. Obese, and I really don't want to be. I have tried every single diet you can think of. First, I tried the Atkins diet...." She continued to explain every diet she had tried and how she failed every single time. Little pearls of tears ran down her round cheeks. Too tired to try and keep it concise, I just stood there and allowed her to lay out her whole problem in every detail.

"I have seen doctors and they have done all the tests. They have found no medical reason for my weight problem. I know it is because of my eating. I have no control, I can't stop. I'm desperate, Doc."

She wiped her eyes and running nose with a white tissue she had tucked underneath the band of her tiny wristwatch.

"It is New Year's morning. When I found myself standing with the fridge door in my hand at five a.m., peering in for something to snack on, I promised myself: this is it. It is 2011. I am not leaving 2011 as a fat girl. This year I am going to get thin. That is why I am here." She said this with determination as she lightly punched her small fist into the palm of her hand. "I need you to help me. Please, Doc."

I felt powerless. Where could I start with this poor girl? She was so hopeful.

"Amelia, it's a difficult problem, but the difficulty is not in *finding* the solution, it is in *practicing* the solution. How shall I put it? The answer is simple math. If the calorie intake in your body is more than you use, you pick up weight. Alternatively, if you use more calories than you take in, you lose weight. Are you still following me clearly?"

She nodded.

"3,500 calories equals one pound. If you want to lose a pound per week, you need to take in 500 calories per day less than your daily usage or requirement. It's actually simple, but not easy. I will refer you to a dietician, but you can start by contacting a reputable weight loss program; they can help you with the calorie content and meals."

"Thanks, Doctor; I appreciate the assistance, but I am actually here today to ask you to prescribe me some medication. Some of my friends took speed and said it helped. Another friend drinks these caffeine drinks to increase her metabolism. Is there something better that I can use? Please, I need something to help me kick-start."

"Well, 'speed' is an amphetamine and there are some medical derivatives for these things, but you need to know that although it might help a bit, you stand a chance of getting very dependent on drugs like those and you will most likely regain your weight again in the long run. Let's start in a different way. I will give you a prescription for a medication you take every day, especially with your main meal of the day. It prevents fat absorption and this will help you more than the other products. See it as a crutch, though. Something to help you start. The real secret is small, balanced meals, daily exercise, and persistence."

I felt good. I felt I had made a connection with her. She appeared to appreciate my care. Ironically, she ended up being the one patient that made that night shift worth it. I had truly helped someone, and most importantly, I felt good about it. For once.

As I drew back the cubicle curtain, I looked up to see Michael standing a few yards away at the doctor's desk. His gaze went from me to Amelia and back to me. Amelia got up and, prescription in hand, walked towards the exit with her knock-kneed shuffle. Michael had a sort of a snarl on his face, as if he had smelled something bad. He said nothing, but his eyes were glued to Amelia until she was gone.

I walked over. "Hi, Michael. Happy New Year."

"Happy New Year to you too!" He pulled me in for a hug and patted my back. He stepped away from the hug, but held onto both my shoulders with his hands and looked at me for a second longer. He gave my shoulders a quick press and then dropped his hands back to his side.

He returned his attention to the charts rolling in from the triage desk. "Interesting lecture, Peter." He leaned in and whispered, "You know it's useless; don't waste your time. Rather fix the ones you can fix." He slowly shook his head while he said it.

I didn't answer, but he'd popped my bubble. *Michael, sometimes you can be a real ass.* I changed the subject. "I have to hand over; I am out on my feet. I need to get to bed."

"How was the New Year's graveyard?"

"You know. All the regulars were here. David Morin, Chad Bishop, Earl Patterson. What can I say? It was draining."

"Such a waste for us to look after those oxygen thieves. It's so freaking useless. In a tougher world like Africa, they'd be gone. Natural selection would get rid of them. But here, the social structure enables them."

What is Michael's problem? Has he always been this harsh? Maybe I'm just too bloody tired.... "A bit feisty so early in the morning. Can we skip the politics?"

"Sure, sure. Have we got any patient transports coming in?"

We did the handover.

"You off now?" Michael asked.

"Yep, like the foreskin said to the rabbi, I'm *off*."

Michael only smiled. It was an old joke. "Are you sleeping all day today?"

"No, just enough to get rid of the worst rust, till noon. I'll go to bed early tonight."

"I work till three. Come over for sundowners tonight."

"Sure. Around sunset?"

"Deal. Cheers, buddy, have a good sleep. Oh, by the way...." He looked me straight in the eye. "I mean it. Have a great New Year."

When I got home New Year's morning, Esmé was already up and waiting for me to arrive. She had made breakfast, and when I slumped into the chair, she brought me a coffee. I looked at the cup, but she quickly said, with a knowing smile, "I know, Dad. It's decaf. You need to get some sleep." Esmé poured herself a cup as well. "Mom's still asleep. So Dad, Happy New Year!" I was amazed at how mature she had become. My little girl was fifteen already. She was exceptionally intelligent, top of her class every year, and stunningly beautiful.

"So, Esmé, what's your New Year's resolution?" I started to eat my breakfast. She sat back in her chair and pulled her knees up to her chest, a habit she'd inherited from her mom.

"Don't know, Dad, but I've been thinking ... I wanna go to med school."

"Med school. Uh huh." I gave a small sigh and cleared my throat. "You'd be great at it. It's a tough job, but you know, I still love it. Some days are a bit tougher.... It's a challenge, but interesting."

"Yeah, I've been thinking, my grades are good enough, and it looks *so* interesting." Her eyes were filled with excitement. *I used to feel like that.*

"You'd be great at it. We can look at the academic prerequisites together, okay?"

"Sure, Dad. Thanks."

I changed the subject. "Gonna get a boyfriend this year? I see the boys can't keep their eyes off you."

"Dad," she blushed. "Some boys are fun, but I like my friends now and I want to get good grades. Anyway, Mom said, 'no serious boyfriends before you're eighteen.' I'm cool with that."

I stared at my little girl, who had turned into a woman right in front of my eyes.

"Any resolutions for you, Dad?"

"Only one: get more sleep. Starting *now.*" I managed to smile through the fatigue. "Thanks for making breakfast. It was lovely."

I dragged my body to the bedroom and snuck into my side of the bed, careful not to wake Sandra.

Joseph Cossman said, “The best bridge between despair and hope is a good night’s sleep.” I only slept for a few hours, but it made me cross that bridge. I woke with a feeling of hope for the year ahead.

The drive towards the west was beautiful. I was excited to see Michael and arrived just before sunset. We sat down on the main level and he poured whiskey.

“Happy New Year!” we toasted as the sun painted the sky pink and the lake disappeared into the dark shadows.

The silence of friendship hung between us. The ice cubes made some restless turns in our glasses. It was very special. I experienced a sense of contentment, calm, and lightness. Michael, however, appeared to have a serious heaviness to his demeanour. I couldn’t place it. Something was gnawing at him.

“Come on, what’s up?”

He contemplated, looking at his glass. “Those fat girls just triggered some memories this morning. I could hear the echoes of my mom’s voice calling, ‘Mickey, Mickey! Can you help mom quickly?’”

I could see his neck stiffen as a shiver ran up his spine. I saw goose bumps on his arm. He took a slow sip of the whiskey. “Sometimes those people make the anger rise in me. Today I even had to step out for a moment.”

Past traumatic event. Flashbacks. Panic. Anger. Depression.

“You know this is clearly PTSD, don’t you? Have you spoken with anyone?”

"Peter, honestly, the crap those psychologists spin irritates the shit out of me. Somehow, no matter who you are, they think you are completely ignorant of psychology. They answer questions with questions and bounce everything back to the patient. Do they really think the rest of the world can't see through their stupid ploy? They don't have any answers, just more questions: How does *that* make you feel? What do *you* think would be the reason? Tell me more about your mother. So your father was away all the time and never really there for you? I can just hear it all play out. Dig. Dig. Dig. Blah. Blah. Blah. Shit. It is only voyeuristic intellectual masturbation for them. I am not wasting my time with that shit." He took another sip of whiskey. He looked at me and smiled. "I 'd rather have a chat with you over a whiskey." I sensed his tone lifting.

"I'm always here for you."

Michael leaned over and toasted my glass. "Of course, Peter, of course."

"Speaking of that girl this morning. Some overweight people have it tough...."

"Sure, it's tough, but it is fixable. Hey!" He looked at me. "'I never said it would be easy.'"

I joined in and we completed the quote in unison. "'I only said it would be worth it.'"

"Cheers to Mae West!" We toasted glasses.

"Anyway, where was I?" Michael continued. "Oh yes: fixable, not easy. Look at the rest of nature. No fat sheep can be found in the wintertime on those Karoo farms. The truth is that people have the knowledge, but not the commitment. They know the answer, but they want the easier way."

"I can see where you are coming from, but you are oversimplifying it a bit, I think—"

"I don't think so. They just need to be more motivated. In this country people are affluent, secure, and happy. There is no true fear. No true driving force. The only marginal motivator is something like 'I wanna look better' or 'I wanna feel better about myself.' After a few hours into a new diet, those motivators evaporate like the morning fog, and then they think, 'You know what? I'll do this next month; I'm actually okay with myself.' They watch some Oprah or Dr. Phil, or they get told by every single psychologist that they should accept who they are, embrace their inner beauty and be content. Then they smile and reach over for the chips and popcorn."

"Sure, but teaching people contentment is also important. In fact, I think it's a good philosophy."

"I disagree, Peter. Teaching contentment in this context is only giving them permission to accept their inherent lack of motivation and never change," he mumbled.

He sat back in the chair as he stared out over the lake, rubbed his chin with his right hand, and said, "People need motivation, not contentment."

The final rays of daylight disappeared and darkness settled over the lake.

He lit a cigarette and offered me one again.

"No, Michael, thank you. I don't smoke anymore. It's only been eight years...."

"I can still see you salivate the second my lighter flashes," he teased.

"Hey, some days saying 'no' to that is my only little sign of strength. Don't knock it. You should quit, you know."

"Save it for your patients. I like smoking. I am no quitter. I'll roll the dice. It won't be smoking that kills me in the end, I'm sure. There are too many other bad habits lining up in front of it." Michael's face appeared harder than before, and inscrutable. "Why do people feel they have the right to offend and even publicly antagonize you about smoking, but no one ever walks up to the fat guy in McDonalds and says, 'Hey, you are too fat. It's gross. Please quit eating the burger and fries in here'?"

"It just isn't socially acceptable to act that way. Maybe society is more tolerant than you."

Michael had a serious look and his voice went up a few decibels.

"Not true, Peter. Not true. Actually being fat is 'not okay,'" he added quotation marks in the air, "in the eyes of society. I think most people dislike fat people; they just don't say it out loud. Even moviemakers and advertisers use society's hatred for the obese to get their own message across subliminally. Let me show you something."

He jumped up and walked to the pen and ink sketch of the Penguin and Batman on display on the living room. "Come, Peter. Look here," he said impatiently. "As you know, this is my pride and joy. This is the original Detective Comics #67, 1942 *First Penguin Cover in Pen and Ink*, and I paid a lot for it. Now this is what I want to show you." He pointed to the sketch of the Penguin himself. "The Penguin in this 1942 depiction is a thin, little, evil person riding on an ostrich. When Tim Burton made the 1989 Batman movie, how did he succeed in changing a penguin, a cute bird, into a hated villain? What characteristic that wasn't present in this 1942 picture did he add to change him into a super villain?"

I looked at the picture carefully. "The penguin is overweight?"

"You got it, Peter. Danny DeVito, playing the Penguin, was made fat and disgusting. The viewers were disgusted by his obese, clumsy gait, his awkwardness, his blubber, and gross gluttony as he gorged himself on fish. In fact, he was so successful that the movie was deemed by critics to be too dark. All Burton did was add blubber and gluttony, and the Penguin became exceptionally repulsive."

"The black saliva drooling down his shirt also helped."

"Yes, I know it was over the top, but you get my point. In society, everybody is friendly and nice to the fat person, but in truth, people despise them. The prejudice is there, but no one admits to it."

"I don't know. I think you're going too far. I think it's more a Michael issue than a society issue."

Michael quietly contemplated my statement for a few moments and finally he said, “Ja Boet!” in his strong Jo’burg accent. “Let’s drop it. We all have issues, eh?” He re-filled our glasses. “To a great 2011!”

We toasted again and then walked downstairs to sit by the fireplace. I crashed at his place. When I drove home the next morning, I hoped 2011 would bring me more personal contentment, and maybe a solution for Sandra and me.

The year would indeed bring many answers; even to questions I never knew to ask.

CHAPTER 22

DAY 45

Nine stacks of five.

There is no God.
I won't pray ever again.
No one is ever going to find me.
No one is looking for me.
Maybe my mom ... maybe not....
It's all for nothing anyway.
Life is shit and then you die.
I wish I would die.
In fact, I wish I was dead.
I am going to stop drinking the water....

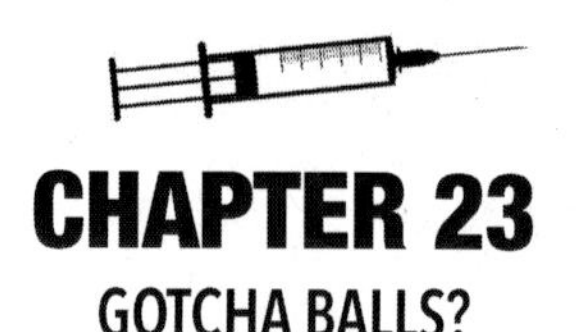

CHAPTER 23

GOTCHA BALLS?

As the winter crossed over into spring, we dusted off our mountain bikes and started to put away the snowboards. It was one of the main attractions of this town: the ski season didn't end until April, but in the valley you could get on your mountain bike and ride single-track trails by March. Michael and I had a yearly tradition of kicking off the biking season by taking a weekend off to go biking and camping.

Michael picked a great spot for us to ride. It was called Gotcha Balls? My nemesis. It involved a long, single-track climb and a very steep, winding descent that completed the loop. Although the climb was usually very tough so early in the season, I was a good grinding climber; however, the exceptionally technical descent always had my number.

To get there, we had to drive an hour out of town. We left on a Friday and set up camp just before nightfall. It was chilly and cool, but refreshing to be out in nature. No one else was crazy enough to camp yet—it was too frosty at night—and so it was extremely quiet. The little lake by the campsite was beautiful, calm, and frozen in the shadowy corners. White birch trees lined the opposite shoreline.

Early on the Saturday morning, I awoke to hear the water boiling by the campfire. Peeking out of my tent, I could see the lid rattling as the water percolated through the coffee. Nothing like the smell of fresh coffee on a frosty morning. I slipped out of the tent and poured myself a cup. Michael was standing by the lake. He leaned against a birch as he smoked a cigarette. The early morning fog hung like a shroud on the water, and the early rays of sun sent searchlight lines through it. Picture perfect.

We had some breakfast and waited for the day to warm up. The track was mostly south facing, so the open areas would be dry, but between the trees it was likely either icy or muddy. On a mountain bike, I preferred the mud, despite the mess.

Our day started with the winding climb. This was no race. It was all about endurance, and so we maintained a steady pace. We kept the gears spinning to warm up our legs for the grind later. I knew what to expect—a day of blood, sweat, and tears—but it was Michael's year to choose the first track. When he chose Gotcha Balls, I realized he had thrown down the gauntlet. I expected this after I crushed him on the previous year's climb (my choice: Rio del Grande). Unbeknownst to him, I spent quite a bit of time on the spin bike during the winter and got my mind straight on the psychology of descent. Michael could fly down a mountain like there was no tomorrow. Fearless. Crazy. Irresponsible....

After about an hour, the climb got really technical. We took a break, had a drink and an energy bar. We clipped in for the grind to the top. The sun beat down on that part of the mountain, where we were out of the trees and the track was dry, loose, and rocky. Pieces of loose rock and branches from the winter littered the track, and it was hard work, much harder than I expected. I thought I was one up on Michael with my winter training, but it appeared he had more strength than last year. He was killing me. I buckled down, cursed myself for being too bloody lazy the past winter, and ground harder. If Michael took the climb, the mountain would be his, since I would never catch him on the down.

I started my personal sport psychology rant in my head. *Pain is only a message. It's only a caution, a warning. You can work through it. You don't have to listen. Weakness comes from fear of pain. Strength comes from embracing it.* And so I kept my legs churning over.

My chest started to burn. I needed to control my breathing better, I thought. My legs were burning to the bone. A deep ache dug into my buttocks and slowly burned into my lower back. My shoulders tightened and a knot formed between the blades. It wasn't going to be my day. Suddenly, I burst my bubble. My legs caved in and resigned like the tripping of a main switch. Powerless.

I tried to keep going as best as I could, but as we rounded a hairpin corner with a beautiful view down to where we started, my fatigue affected my balance and the loose shale shifted as I turned. For a brief second I thought I was going to fall down the mountain, but I regained my balance at the last moment and threw myself back towards the hillside. I put my foot out to steady me.

It was a close call. I watched as the loose rocks fell down the mountain to my right. I pulled my slipped hind wheel back onto the track as I looked down over the side.

"Watch out! Helluva penalty for failure there, buddy," Michael commented.

I conceded victory to Michael. "My legs are dead. I'm blown. Let's take a moment." We sat down and got our breath back. The view was astounding. "I hate weak days," I mumbled.

"I hate weakness."

"Sorry to disappoint you."

"Ah geez, don't be so sensitive. I'm not talking about you at all. My mind has been on some of the guys we work with who are weak. Indecisive. I did a shift with Andy Miller yesterday."

I nodded knowingly. Andy Miller was a fellow emergency doctor who was renowned amongst the emergency doctors for being very slow and unable get through a large workload. If you ended up on a shift after him, you expected to be handed huge backlogs and lots of patients.

"What's with Andy?" Michael continued. "If you can't make decisions, then emergency medicine isn't for you. The essence of the job is making a decision fast, without having all the facts at your disposal. Call it as you see it. Trust your gut and be willing to take responsibility for it. He is just so indecisive; every patient gets investigated to the yin yang. He doesn't want to make decisions."

"I think he's just a perfectionist. He doesn't want to make a mistake."

"None of us do, but the wheels of the whole health industry will grind to a bloody halt if we all were to practice his sort of medicine. Holy mackerel, be an engineer or an accountant if you want it neat and precise. Medicine is a game of odds and estimates, risks and benefits, ifs and buts. It's never precise. You've got to be willing to make mistakes to practise it properly."

"Easy for you to say, Michael. You're a genius."

He laughed. "It's not about the mistakes. It's about making decisions—to err is human. Like my dad. He fought a war for a senseless cause, in my opinion, but he believed in it and he was decisive. As in any war, they had to make judgement calls, and we know all about some of the terrible decisions that were made. But they called it and did what they thought needed to be done. Right or wrong, they were decisive. That's the person I aspire to be: the one with the balls to make the call and do what needs to be done. That's who my dad was and what I most respect him for.

Speaking of balls ... did you bring yours today?" He winked at me and got on the bike again.

We ground the last twenty minutes to the top. A spectacular 360-degree view of the British Columbia mountain ranges welcomed us. I felt small and insignificant in the great expanse. We had lunch there while the intimidating descent to the valley patiently waited for me, like a monster snarling, 'What goes up must come down.' I could feel the nerves stirring up my pulse rate. I felt a clumsy little tremor.

Michael looked at me. "You look tense. Nervous. Don't let it get to your head. Just let go and roll with it. Open up those brakes, let the wheels turn. You know if you grip those hydraulic brakes tightly, you'll lock up and slide. Finger them lightly, but embrace the speed. Mario Andretti said, 'If everything still feels under control, you're just not going fast enough.'"

I smiled. Michael was insane. "I think you don't wanna brake because you're in denial. You think you're in control, but you don't want to touch the brakes, since it will only confirm that you're not."

"Come on, you little wuss! It's not called Gotcha Balls for nothing!" Michael got up and lowered his bike seat right down to the frame.

Having the seat so low enabled you to get through the steep sections more easily. When it got really steep, you could straighten out your arms completely and lift your buttocks off and behind the seat. "With your balls hanging over the back wheel," as Michael explained it the first time. Your seat would be nestled nearly right under your chest. If you did not get your body weight all the way back, the steep pitch would easily throw you over the handlebars. We clipped in and started to roll down.

Michael embraced the track and leaned in. I let him go ahead, and he yelled back, "Just ... let ... go!" as the dust shot up from his back wheel and he plummeted out of sight.

I took a deep breath in and out, turned the music in my earphones to the max, and started to ride down. As Michael's words rang in my mind, I slowly opened my clenching fists and allowed the brakes to release completely. The trance beat of "Sandstorm" blasted through my head. I embraced the rhythm and the techno beat synchronized with the curvy single track down. The momentum and adrenaline blended with the beat. I was flying. It was surreal; like an aspirin, my fear dissolved, and I accelerated down the mountain, ignoring the consequences. It was exhilarating. I slid into a few corners and cleared a ledge. When I realized how fast I was going, I was at the point of no return. I approached a sharp turn, but there was no way I could stop or even slow down for it. *Ah, fuck it,* my brain yelled. The final sharp hairpin was a hard right-handed turn with a cliff ledge that provided a significant penalty if I didn't make the corner. I approached at a menacing speed. I put all my weight into the turn. I resisted the temptation to look down the mountain and ignored the cliff on my left completely. I swivelled my head to my right, looking round the corner, trying to keep my full focus on the track ahead of me. Michael always said, "You've got to look where you wanna go, otherwise you're gonna end up where you were looking."

I heard rocks tumble into oblivion behind me as I cleared the corner. The adrenaline rushed through me like the tremors of an earthquake. "Woo-hoo!" I yelled. "Yeah!" The next section evened out, and with all the speed I had built up over the last few turns, I unexpectedly caught up with Michael.

The track dipped away again and swooped down the single-track switchbacks. We were travelling faster than I had ever gone on a section of trail. The trail was tacky with great grip for the tires. I could really lie into the corners and trust my tires to grip. As we descended, the trail got drier and dustier, causing us to slide into the dusty corners of the switchbacks, shooting plumes of dust down the mountain. We were flying. Little bumps became launch pads. When we cleared the last big corner, I was, to my surprise, still keeping up with Michael. He pulled out all the stops, and I was sticking to him, pushing myself to the limit. I saw Michael launch himself over a ledge. He got great air, but then a big dust cloud rose. *Crash.* I had a millisecond to change my trajectory. I aimed for the right-hand side of the dust cloud to miss him. I stuck the landing and slammed on the brakes, skidding to a halt. Looking back, I saw Michael lying on his back and heard an eerie laugh.

"Aaahh! Ha ha ha ... aaagh ... wicked. That hurt, man. Ugh ... ha ha...."

"Are you okay?" I yelled.

"Yeah, maybe cracked a rib or two...."

"What happened?"

"Struck a loose rock on landing."

He rolled to his side and got up, covered in dust. His sunglasses had come off and his whole face was covered in pale powder. The dust-free areas around his eyes, where the sunglasses had been, showed his olive skin. He looked as if he were wearing a face-mask. He had a wide grin. Joker face.

"That was awesome. I got the up; you got the down! Who would've thought? Hey, let's get a beer."

We rode the last few kilometres of flat track to camp at a cool down pace.

"You sure you're okay? You gave me a fright there."

"I'm okay. Just a rib, I think. Now you know I'm human."

I couldn't take the smile off my face for the rest of the day.

My best ride ever.

CHAPTER 24

CAMPFIRE

We got to our campsite, and Michael popped a few ibuprofens for his aching ribs. I quickly checked him out. He did seem tender on the ribcage but had no other injuries.

We got the fire going and then washed the dust off in the freezing lake water. Wrapped in large towels and blankets, we opened a few beers, started a huge campfire and relived a glorious ride.

"You truly conquered your fear today, Peter. You were flying down the mountain."

"I wouldn't say 'conquered,' only ignored. I just blocked out all the warning signals and voices yelling at me to slow down by turning up the beat and rolling with the mountain track. It felt as if fear was yelling something at me from a jetty far away while I was sitting in the middle of a lake. As if I heard the echoes, but could not hear the message."

"Fear: the only true human emotion and motivator. It's the reason we do everything, it's the driving force behind evolution. It's the essence of being a human. We get petrified—man, I love that word—and we have to break through it. Our mission in life is to conquer fear, to break its hold. You did it today, Peter. It was an evolutionary step. That little chink you made in fear's armour today will change you forever."

"Well, it felt great, let me tell you."

"Now that you've done it once, you won't have the same fear in the future. Knowledge dissolves fear. We crave knowledge to conquer our fears. Only when we cast the light under the bed, the fear of the monster disappears. Human beings will do anything to conquer their fears; it's why we become religious, or why gods are created. People need someone who knows the future: an all-knowing ally who will carry them through the valley of death. A friend on the other side. It's the fear of the unknown, the future, death, and hell that drives human beings to religion."

The campfire crackled, and a big stump exploded, sending sparks into the star-filled sky. We followed them trekking up.

"People do find happiness in religion, though. Could you truly say that you are happy without it, Michael?"

Michael contemplated the question for a while. "Blindly believing in something my mind tells me does not exist isn't ever going to work for me. I'd love a big brother who could make life wonderful for me. But I can't convince myself of it, and hoping something exists is never going to make it true. For me, happiness depends on your definitions. Many people have certain ideas of what and when they will be happy. When they reach those goals, they define themselves as happy. I don't. I am. I accept life and embrace whatever it brings. I rise to its challenges; I laugh when it defeats me. It's a chess game—I love the game whether I am winning or losing. If you define happiness as 'winning,' you are destined for a miserable life. If you define happiness as the opportunity to play, then life is great. I think the essence of life's spice exists on the knife's edge, the outside of the envelope. It's all about feeling alive, not about feeling happy, and I think you feel most alive at the moment you face death."

I laughed. "You must have felt very alive today during your spectacular wipe-out, then."

"I did and I do."

"It sounds like a death wish."

"It's the opposite. Call it an 'alive' wish. When facing death, I truly feel alive. However, I do realize I have the luxury of throwing the dice, as it is only me who pays the penalty."

"But you are still accountable for your actions. You are not an island. What you do impacts those around you. Especially at work. If you make mistakes, someone else pays for it."

"I agree, but here's the rub." He leaned forward, and in the light of the fire I could see a sly smile sneak across his face. "Do you know why I have never been sued, never been reprimanded, never been warned or cautioned, or why none of my cases end up on the review rounds?"

"No, please tell me, please. I beg you, your Highness, oh perfect one," I taunted.

"I believe people can only assign blame if you are open to accepting it. It's like humiliation. You can taunt me, but you cannot humiliate me. You can load me with tasks, but you cannot make me feel stressed about it. You can blame me, but you cannot make me feel guilty. Not accepting the accusations mirrors them back to the sender. The sender immediately realizes that the accusation did not have the desired impact. It unnerves them, and they retract. When you project the aura that you are infallible, people start believing it, and they eventually stop looking for mistakes. It is not that I don't make mistakes, but people believe that I must be right; therefore, I am."

"I can't decide if you have a god complex or a form of extreme narcissism."

"Well, God is a narcissist. It's all about Him, isn't it?" he mocked. "Seriously, God is a great example. People define God as being 'right,' and thus if He gives the 'wrong' answer, then...." He shrugged. "They re-examine their question. Example: The farmer prays for rain. A fire consumes the farm. Instead of being angry at God, the religious farmer determines God is sending him the message to farm elsewhere. God stands above judgement; because God is right, we must be wrong if we have a different opinion. God can get away with murder. In fact, when the Jews' God killed all the firstborn boys of the Egyptians, it wasn't deemed 'murder' because God did it. When Hitler did the same to the Jewish children, they felt differently. If lightning strikes a person, we call it an act of God, but we would never call God a murderer. The more godlike you are, the more you can get away with."

"Well, it appears those beers are talking now. Your last girlfriend must've yelled, 'Oh my God' one too many times. Seriously, I see where you're coming from, but please do not repeat that shit to anyone else, Michael—you'll end with your godlike ass in a psych ward."

Michael pulled the whiskey bottle out and poured. "Amen. How are you, Peter?"

"Shit, where do I start? Let's just say things are tough between Sandra and me. The spark is gone." I threw a few more logs onto the fire.

"Anything more specific going on?"

"No, that's exactly it. It's the intangibles, the non-specifics. Something is missing. Gone. Lost. We're detached. I don't know where it's going. The whole thing is adrift. Directionless. I find it boring, and I used to be the boring one. I don't really know how we got here. It used to be fun. We used to have fun. I am just disenchanted; the shine has rubbed off.... Fuck, it's impossible to put my finger on it."

"I don't want to place blame or pick sides in this. I've known both of you from the start and care for you both, but Peter, those feelings may just be projection.

You have been quite distracted lately. Down in the dumps a bit. Maybe you're projecting personal negativity onto your relationship."

"You're probably right. I do feel I have lost perspective on life lately. I am generally irritable, frustrated. I have had those feelings of impending doom frequently. Grim Reaper has been entering the room with me lots lately. I can feel his shadow following me, lurking in the corners and behind curtains. I am constantly in a battle, and I feel like he's winning."

"Death is part of life. In fact, death is the only certain thing in life. If you make that your battle, he will always win."

"Today was the best I felt in months. I felt alive for once. No feeling of doom at all. It could just be the whole midlife thing, but it's such a bloody easy thing to blame. If anything screws up emotionally and you're somewhere around the forty or fifty mark, it's a midlife crisis. We round up the usual suspects, and it prevents us from looking at what is truly going on. It's the patsy: 'Oh, don't worry. It's your midlife crisis.' I have never trusted an easy answer. If it's easy, I'm looking for the catch."

"Listen, I don't know what's going on behind closed doors, and unlike you," Michael winked, "I am not such a voyeur. I hope you guys get it sorted. Maybe this is the time Layla from Blouberg referred to. Maybe you two are in different phases of your life. Maybe you need to re-analyse what you want from life. You need a break from reality, an escape."

"Isn't that exactly what we are doing out here?"

"Maybe. But I am referring to a complete rip from reality. I'm talking *Vegas,* baby!"

"I don't know. Not really my scene, I guess."

Michael laughed. "Obviously you don't do Vegas like I do Vegas."

We left it at that.

We drank a last nightcap of beautiful old single-malt Oban whiskey. Michael started reminiscing about some of the good old Blouberg beach parties and the days in residency, but I was drifting off to sleep. His voice and the memories lulled me.

CHAPTER 25

GRIM REAPER

After our weekend away, I really thought I had a new lease on life. It was as if the sun was pushing its rays through the thunderclouds.

On my first shift back, I visited the doctor's lounge to pick up my mail. I reviewed reports on inpatient care and discharge summaries for the patients we admitted. As I paged through the reports, I slowly sat down. I could hear the chilling echo of his laughter in the back of my mind. Grim Reaper had made his calls again.

Earl Patterson—the grumpy old guy who didn't want me to call him 'sir'—died in hospital from respiratory failure.

Mrs. Catherine Campbell—the eighty-seven-year-old lady whom I admitted with a broken hip four months earlier—had been readmitted. She struggled to cope alone at home. She fell again and fractured a few ribs. Halstead, the pain specialist, gave her some intercostal blocks for the fractures that would've provided some pain blockage, but she must have suffered. She had contracted a pulmonary embolism and died. She was a frail, lovely old lady. I recalled her strong hopes of "joining her husband in Heaven." Well good for her, I thought. She really did not want to continue. At least he took someone who wanted to go.

And then strike three. On the front page of the newspaper lying on the coffee table was the story of Doherty Christy, a twenty-four-year-old who had jumped off the Peterson Bridge. The article was an emotional appeal and attack on the incompetence of the mental health network in our region. It said the system had failed Doherty and asked for better screening systems to be put into place. The family and friends interviewed all agreed. Immediately I became upset about the shifting of responsibility, a common phenomenon lately. If the family did not notice her mental health issues, then the system would never pick it up. As I looked at the picture again, I recognized her face. Chilling goose bumps rose in my neck. She was the one who had accompanied her friend to the ER on New Year's morning. I never saw her as a patient, but I recalled those two bubbly, chatty, big girls.

Grim Reaper's laughter echoed in the shadows of my mind. *This will never end.*

A freaky chill hit me when I heard, "Code blue emergency department, code blue emergency department."

I ran into the trauma resuscitation area, where the ambulance guys had pulled the patient onto the emergency bed. The report came quickly. The middle-aged homeless person was found in cardiac arrest on the park bench right in front of the hospital. He looked familiar to me.

The triage nurse entered to get the patient's details from ambulance staff and said, "Oh boy. It's David Morin. I didn't even know he had been discharged. He was here this morning. Caroline triaged him just before shift change. I'll get his chart. He had some muscle pains or something."

He wasn't breathing and CPR was in progress. He had no pulse, and his heart rhythm was a flat line.

"How long have you been going?" I asked the ambulance personnel as I indicated to the respiratory therapist that she should get ready for me to intubate him.

"We've been going only for a few minutes, Doc. We found him on your lawn here in front. We don't know how long he's been there, though, 'cause he was sitting on the bench, and a passer-by thought he looked 'odd' because he was sitting asleep. When the police arrived and they shook him to wake him up, he rolled over onto the grass. He was unconscious or dead. They couldn't feel a pulse. They called security to get a stretcher, but it's not in security's job description, so they called the ambulance. Anyway, it's a long story."

"Who started CPR?"

The ambulance staff looked at each other. "When we got there ... let's just say technically the police did, but there is CPR and there is CPR." I got the message. Good CPR had only been done for the last few minutes.

"So do we have any idea how long he could have been unconscious?"

The ambulance guy looked at his watch and paperwork. "Probably at least thirty to forty minutes."

"And meds?"

"He's had one milligram atropine and EPI—two rounds."

"What was his initial rhythm?"

"Asystole all the way."

I intubated him and turned to the respiratory therapist. "Let's quickly check the tube placement." I listened to the chest and felt comfortable the tube was in the right place. "Let's get a chest x-ray quickly to check."

A new person took over CPR, as the previous one was getting tired and sweaty from the continuous work.

I walked round to the end of the bed, and the nurse handed me the chart for his visit earlier. Michael had seen him. A diagnosis of musculoskeletal back pain was made, and he received an intramuscular injection of an anti-inflammatory before he left. Nothing indicated why he would be in cardiac arrest.

I was working on all possible causes in my mind, and asked the nurse to give him a reversal agent for morphine, in case David's condition was due to an overdose—we all knew he had addiction issues, so it was worth a shot. I did a quick mental recap: *Cardiac arrest. Unknown cause. Possible overdose. Probable respiratory arrest leading to cardiac arrest. Rhythm asystole. Intubated and ventilated. CPR going for*—I looked at my watch—*an hour.* Tick. Tick. Tick.

I heard Grim Reaper's eerie whisper in my right ear. "I think you should call it." It felt so real that I looked to my right. Michael was standing there. Our eyes met and he held my stare. His eyes said the same thing.

I was the team leader. *If he came back now, he'd be a vegetable.* That was my final thought in the case of David Morin.

Halstead was on call for ICU and walked into the room with his entire ego. He scanned the scene, looked straight at me, and said in his loud, confrontational voice, "What are you doing here?"

"Don't worry, Halstead, I'm calling it. Stop CPR. Time of death: 10:21. Thank you, everyone. It was a great effort."

Halstead turned on his heels and walked straight out again. On his way out, his shoulder brushed Michael's. Halstead walked his line, and Michael stood his ground.

I turned to the social worker in the room. "David had a friend, another addict. They travelled together and always came to emergency together. Craig something?"

"Villaincourt," she said.

"Will you notify him?"

"Well, they're homeless, so I don't know where to find him, but I'll check with the men's shelters and see what I can do. It's strange when you know their names, isn't it?" She must've seen the defeat on my face. Was it that obvious? I didn't even know her name. She reached out and lightly touched my folded forearms with her hand. "You tried your best."

The kindness broke something inside me. I excused myself quickly; Michael covered for me as I slipped out.

There was no one else on the roof. I walked to the railing and had to release the pressure inside. I looked out over the city. Mount Paul looked silently down at the river as it cut a valley through the rock. *Persistence and time. Water is stronger than rock.*

At the top of my voice, I yelled into the night. "I give up! Okay? You fucking win! Okay? Just leave me alone!" The words disappeared into the night, drowned out by the continuous humming of the roof's ventilation turbines. Empty and defeated, I returned to the emergency room.

The rest of my shift, I was completely unsettled. To crown it all, we had another unsuccessful resuscitation. It was a fifty-six-year-old man with cardiac arrest, probably a heart attack. It was a valiant effort by the ambulance staff, and we had some return of blood flow and a heartbeat for a short while, but it wasn't to be. He clung to those feeble signs of life for a few minutes, but as the adrenaline ran out, it all ended.

A large family arrived, and since his death came unexpectedly, the wife wailed and cried and threw herself on her husband, yelling, "No! No! No!" She shook his shoulders and tried to claw him back from the grip of the reaper. The four daughters cried and hollered in a huddle. The brother tried to comfort the wife, and the Catholic mother stood with a little cross in hand and cried, waiting for the priest to arrive.

Tragic.

I felt nothing. Numb. Comfortably numb.

"Hello, is there anybody in there?"

I was worse than numb, actually. The deathbed scene irritated me. The family was making noise and obstructing emergency patient flow because they were blocking a bed.

It wasn't me anymore. I felt completely detached from the Peter I knew before.

When I mentioned this to Michael, he said, "Well, Peter, as doctors we're supposed to have empathy, but if you lose it, I'll welcome you to the dark side. You know me. I actually never cared too much for people. They amuse me. Ironically, having no real empathy keeps me objective. It gives me better perspective. I think I can make better decisions, be a better clinician. So don't grieve your loss of empathy. Your decisions will become clearer from this point on."

I took the words at face value. They were meant to comfort me, but they filled me with unease. I walked to my car, got in, and sat there for half an hour.

Was I losing my humanity? How does one regain such a thing?

Where do I go from here? Home?

I turned the ignition key.

CHAPTER 26

DAY 60

Twelve stacks of five.

She took a sip of water. *Wasn't there a time that I wanted to stop drinking the water?* It was all fuzzy. *Drinking water is just about the only thing to do here.*

"That's not true, honey," she thought she heard her mother say.

"Let's make a list!" she said. "Isn't that what you would say, Mom?" She looked at her bed where her coat was propped up like a person. "There *is* the walking. Did my ten laps today! There is the visit to the body function container, as our host calls it. There is the wonderful meal of one banana and eleven almonds and thirteen cashew nuts that I will eat around midday. Of course, we can drink from the endless supply of water. There's the architectural corner; I've been able to build that bottle pyramid pretty high. It looks beautiful when the afternoon sun hits it. Oh, the weather, you ask? It is cool at night, but I think it's cozy. I've always liked to sleep with a warm body and a cool, frosty nose, you know. Any entertainment? Well, last week a bear rubbed up to the corner. I wasn't actually scared, but it was pretty noisy when he scratched his back against the wall. It was funny, 'cause I hoped he could get in—then I could have left! You think the grizzly would've let me go? What happened to him, you ask? He banged that ladder down, and the noise scared him away.... Well, that sort of wraps it up, Mom. Nice to hear from you. Glad you came to say hello!"

The voice boomed, "Strip."

It was the first time in a while that the voice had made her jump. *Must've been the nice chat with mom that got me side-tracked.*

She did as commanded and slowly walked to the corner.

The spotlight came on and she stepped forward and looked down. She knew this routine well.

Ooh. That's pretty close.

But as expected, the loud buzzer went off.

She shuffled to her mat and started to dress slowly.

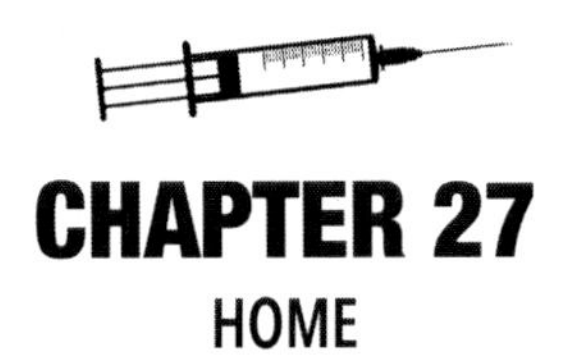

CHAPTER 27

HOME

Sandra's eyes were icy pale. Her eye colour could change significantly with her emotions, from a soothing crystal blue to an icy pale white. Most of the time, I found them unfathomable, but I knew what it meant when they became a sultry, seductive blue. However, I hadn't seen that for a long time. Only the icy pale eyes were present lately.

Although Sandra could easily fool me with her body language and words, I had learned that her eyes were always truthful, and her lips even more so. When her lips thinned out, she was angry with me. When her lips were full and soft, they confirmed things were okay. In recent months I had not once tasted those full, soft lips. They were hiding somewhere with the sultry blue eyes.

It wasn't the first time we had been through such spells, but it was the longest. Sex and intimacy had disappeared.

I struggled with my sexual desire for Sandra. It was like a beast that would slowly gain strength and unexpectedly break free from my control. Like a bull in a cage, I would start stomping around, seeing red everywhere. I would reach a point where it all got too much and I'd ignite. Although my Buddhist counsellor advised against it, I tried to control these desires by sweeping them under the proverbial carpet and ignoring them, only to find myself losing my temper at work. I despised the fact that this demon had power over me. Everyone battles their own demons, I guess.

Sandra used to notice when I was struggling with this and would smooth things over with sex or intimacy. I was convinced she wasn't always in the mood and probably even faked orgasms like I heard women did, but I wouldn't have known the difference.

Either way she would break the spell. During one of these make-up sessions, I noticed that she avoided kissing me. When I forced a kiss, I was blindsided by a very angry, thin-lipped response.

This posed the question: Did I really want to know? Did I want the truth, or did I want to believe the lie as long as its message was "I love you"?

I never forced a kiss again.

"Hi. I'm home." I hollered up the stairs after another energy-sapping day shift. I felt completely drained. My feet burned and ached in protest when I stepped out of the car. Esmé was away for the weekend, and it was only Sandra and me at home. The tension was palpable.

We only had each other to talk to.

We had nothing to say.

I got the mail at the front door and I wondered why I was the one to pick up the mail at our front door, after working all day, and why Sandra, who had her butt stuck to the couch at home all day, could not make the two-yard effort.

"I'm up here," Sandra's voice came down the hardwood stairs from the split-level. I walked into my office by the front door and dumped all my mail in the inbox on my desk. Sandra got a bill from yet another credit card company I hadn't been aware of. *Holy.* The bloody debt was getting under my skin. We had tons of bills, our shared credit card was maxed out, and now another card appeared. Was I only good for bringing in the dollars? Apparently I wasn't even bringing in enough. She had developed the talent of outspending my earning ability. *Congratulations, you win.*

I walked up the stairs to the main living area, where Sandra was lying on the couch paging through one of those celeb-drivel magazines. Her head was propped up on the armrest and her feet up on the other side of the two-seater. Again she stunned me with her natural beauty and sex appeal. Her glowing blond hair softly rolled off the end of the couch. She was still gorgeous. But the moment lasted only a second before it became fuel for my bonfire of irritation. We hadn't had sex for at least two months ... the bonfire turned into wildfire quickly.

Breathe in, breathe out, Peter. Let it go. My meditation counsellor's mantra.

She didn't respond at all as I walked in the room; she only turned the page. I didn't recognize the dickhead on the cover, but the headline was "Break-up—all revealed. Exclusive pictures."

I couldn't see the point in reading that crap. Oh so-and-so was wearing this and that and kissing this joe-blow while actually dating that jack-shit. *Oooh.* Enthralling. It was fabulous to see that Sandra had added that particular piece of fuck-all knowledge to her head today. Never mind I was busting my ass trying to keep people alive.

I dropped the bill for the brand-new credit card on her lap. "What is that about? Don't we have enough debt?" I asked.

She didn't even look at me. She glanced at the bill from under the magazine and then continued to read the magazine. "Oh, that. My other cards weren't working, so I got this one."

I could feel the surge rising in me. Her tone truly got to me. It implied she deserved to be the lazy ass lying on the couch, that it was my duty to provide, and that I wasn't even doing a particularly good job because the other cards "weren't working."

Why did I always end up this way with her? She was always one-upping me.

Heat rushed up my neck into my face. I felt like pouncing on the couch and choking the living daylights out of her. *If I did put my fingers around her throat and squeezed with all my power, how long would it take before she stopped scratching at me? Would I have enough strength to keep her down till the end? Would my arms be long enough to keep her hands away from my face and eyes? I would probably chicken out halfway through—*

What the hell was I thinking?

I still stood motionless next to the couch.

Silence hung.

Should I finally blow the whole marriage to pieces, or should I have a shower? *Tough call.*

Maybe Sandra was right. She always seemed to win the arguments. Maybe Michael was right. Maybe it was my own projections that caused these paranoid thoughts. Was it my depression and paranoia?

Could it all be me? Had I missed something, some little detail? But then, did I really want to know? Was I just done with it all?

"Who do you think is going to pay this bill?"

She looked at me. Her eye contact was full of electricity—the kind, incidentally, that connected to your testicles in a torture chamber. She brought her feet down from the armrest and sat up straight. She never cowered from a challenge; maybe that's why I loved her. Like a hungry boxer going for the title, she'd jump into the fight right away. She could be feisty. Her tactics were to forcefully enter the ring, immediately claim dominance, quickly find the weak spot in my argument, and keep pounding it till victory was hers. No matter how well I premeditated my arguments, she had a knack for cracking them wide open and flipping them upside down. Before I had a chance to recover or rethink it, I'd be knocked out, or the white towel would be thrown into the ring by 'my team.' My team's motto was "Lose the fight to win the war."

That day I felt careless and hopeless, but defiant. I felt like I had nothing to lose, although everything was on the line. I had a strange strength. Only the truth would suffice. *Truth or Bust.*

Sandra sensed something different in my demeanour and held back for a few moments. She didn't take the bait, initially. "I know it's not about the card. What's eating you, Peter?"

Point of no return....

"Are you screwing around? Are you having an affair?"

"Oh, for crying out loud, Peter!" She threw her head back wildly and her arms in the air as she jumped into the fighting ring. Her voice shot up a few decibels and she attacked like always. Attack is always the best defence, isn't it?

Calmly my thought announced itself to me. *That's it. I think I am done here.*

Suddenly I could see right into 'the Matrix.' I could see through the illusion of our marriage and face the reality of the separate lives we were already living under the same roof. It wasn't about her or about what she had or had not done. It wasn't even about blame. I recognized the reality. I couldn't fight for the illusion anymore.

All these thoughts were circling in the depths of my mind, like a frenzy of sharks assessing the blonde prey splashing and thrashing on the surface.

"There is no spoon," I said. One of the best movie quotes of all time.

Sandra, who had been ranting continuously, stopped mid-sentence with a quizzical expression.

"What? Are you even listening to a single word I am saying?" She scratched her head in an irritated fashion and found her train of thought. "Anyway, where was I? Are we never getting past this? Always suspicious! Always thinking I am sneaking around behind your back. I've told you. It is your issue, not mine, but this is seriously getting to me now. This is enough. Stop this BS! You are depressed and freaking paranoid. You are projecting your insecurities on me. You feel insecure in yourself and someone must be to blame. Oh, it must be because Sandra is sleeping around. No, Peter. It is your problem, your issue, your insecurity. You sort it out."

She felt she had annihilated me in a few seconds. She walked to the kitchen and then stopped in her tracks. She wasn't done yet.

"You know what, Peter? You think you want the truth, but you don't. You want me to be screwing around to confirm your suspicions. You don't want the actual facts. You just want your fantasy of deceit to be true. You want proof that you're not paranoid. But we all know. You. Are. Paranoid. Accept it."

It's all about accepting reality, isn't it?

She continued to rant. "Get over it! You will never believe the facts. You will always believe I am cheating, but that you just haven't been able to prove it yet. Just give it a break already. You suck the life out of this marriage."

I think it's time that I say something.

"*Life*? There is no life to be sucked. It's dead already. DNR—Do Not Resuscitate. It's been dead for months, hell, maybe for years. Let's call a spade a spade."

That felt good! My punch had hit something solid. Now I had to go through with it. My brain raced. *Turn and walk away, turn and walk, turn and walk.* I turned and walked into the bedroom.

I took a weekend bag and started packing. *Are you sure about this, buddy?* It was a tug of war in my mind. Stop, go, stop, go. My arms were siding with the 'go' team and I kept packing. My legs were on the other side. They were filled with lead. My knees had a slight tremor and wanted to buckle.

Sandra was talking. I knew she was, because I could see those thin lips and hands moving. No sound. It was quite amusing, actually. I could see she was getting worked up because I wasn't responding to her arguments. I heard the sounds, the tones, and the anger like a familiar melody, but not the words. There was only one way from there.

I looked at her face.

Frozen, icy pale eyes. Thin lips.

That's all the confirmation I needed. *Cheers.*

The smirk stuck to my face and I walked down the stairs. My legs felt numb and I had limited control over them, but it seemed they'd finally changed their allegiance. Like an elastic snapping, I only felt release.

Sandra yelled. She was out of control. "Why are you smiling? What the hell are you doing? Are you quitting?"

I stopped walking and turned towards her. I made eye contact and held her stare till she quietened down. All I felt was certainty.

"Accept what is, Sandra. Those are your words. You were right. I should have looked at the reality of my situation. I should've accepted a long time ago that there is nothing for me here anymore. No need to wage a war for something that isn't there. I'm not saying it's lost forever. I'm saying it isn't here. I need to leave."

She stood there. Frozen. The ice in her eyes started to thaw, leaving silver streaks on her cheeks.

I got in my car and drove off without knowing where I was going. I called Michael, and he knew immediately that it was serious. I asked him if I could stay at his place for a while.

"Sure, Peter. I'll pour the whiskey. Sounds like a rough one."

The tremors had settled by the time I got there. I could breathe again.

After a few drinks, Michael said, "We need to visit Layla! Remember her advice twenty years ago?"

CHAPTER 28

VEGAS, BABY!

Two days later we landed in the capital of hedonism—Las Vegas. We booked into a great hotel overlooking the Strip and popped a bottle of champagne minutes later.

"What happens in Vegas, stays in Vegas," Michael toasted.

"Ask no questions, hear no lies," I replied.

"Man, those are terribly corny quotes. We need to do *way* better than that. Let's get a drink." Michael poured the bubbly.

A hedonistic spree began that crossed all boundaries in the sole pursuit of fun. No morals, no conscience, no consequences, if it was ever possible. No negotiations with Michael. I was told, "Let it go, just go with the flow."

Michael became the tour guide, organizer, and entertainment co-ordinator. He loved it, and he knew Vegas like the palm of his hand. When I asked him how he knew everything about the place, he just bounced my quote back at me. "Ask no questions, hear no lies!"

We glided through the casinos and saw a couple of shows, but I was in Vegas to escape and this we did on the second day. Late afternoon, the limo picked us up from the hotel. It took the road west towards the Mountain Springs range. We drove into the sunset like an old cowboy movie. The horizon signalled red—a sign of what the night had in store.

As Michael refilled my glass with champagne, he informed me that prostitution was actually illegal in Las Vegas. Knowing that I was a bit of a stickler for the law, we were leaving the city for a night 'over the hump' in Pahrump, where brothels were legal. Thinking of what lay ahead, I was full of sexual anticipation, but when I considered the physical details of it, I cringed. My idea of a brothel was hordes of drooling, sweaty men and prancing, bleached-blonde girls with silicone boobs. The sleaziness, the talk of money, the fear of disease, the guilt of betrayal, and the shame of being so desperate for sex were all rolled into one. I feared seeing clean, tiled floors, easily cleanable surfaces, and the faint smell of bleach. All artificial. All superficial. A staged reality sex show. The girls lining up. Playing God, judge, and jury. Picking a girl. Picking a themed room. 'Do you want a Jacuzzi with that? Visa or MasterCard?'

It all repelled me. I wanted to bail, but then I smiled at my own hypocrisy. *Maybe you shouldn't come looking for reality in Vegas, you idiot. Just enjoy the moment.*

Michael knew me better than I thought.

Some of the world's most famous brothels were situated in Pahrump, and Michael had made arrangements for us at a very private, high-end ranch. We were welcomed, and it appeared our host knew Michael personally. There was a clear glint of recognition in her eyes, but then maybe she just enjoyed looking at him. We walked into a lounge and bar area. I saw no other men. The only patrons were Michael and I. Four beautiful ladies were sitting at the bar. They were dressed very elegantly in evening gowns and sipping on flutes of champagne. It had the atmosphere of an old English gentleman's club. Soft music was in the background, a low fire crackled in the fireplace. Deep leather seating, thick carpet, and the soft hue of wall lighting on paintings filled the space. Michael smiled knowingly, and all my anxieties and preconceived reservations disappeared. The ladies were very pleasing company. We chatted and laughed over a few drinks at the bar. After a while, two of the girls sweetly excused themselves. Incidentally, the two remaining were the ones that I liked the most anyway. How naïve of me, of course. These people know what they're doing; they figured out quickly where our interests lay. It felt very natural and real. I later learned in escort circles that there was an actual term for this: GFE—girlfriend experience. I loved it. I loved the flow of the night. It appealed to my ego, not my wallet. I felt as if I had actually charmed the ladies. I realized cognitively that it was artificial, but who cared? It felt real, not cheap. I'm sure it wasn't cheap either, but I wouldn't know; for Michael didn't even allow me to bring my wallet to Vegas.

We dined, and the wine flowed. The evening took a more sensual turn, and the four of us ventured into the adjacent bedroom. The sex spiralled towards a re-enactment of our night of ecstasy twenty years before. Four naked bodies in full exploration mode, me being the least experienced one in the room.

Ironically, the pinnacle of my ecstatic male fantasy did not rip me from reality but rather had the opposite affect. It left me missing Sandra more than I had ever missed her before. I tried to reach climax, but I could not be released. Exhausted and frustrated with myself, I rolled away on the large bed. The brunette—I'll call her Busty— realized I was distracted and frustrated. She softly whispered in my ear, "Don't sweat it, honey. Relax, watch. If you feel like it, join us again. You're trying too hard to get there. Let it come to you." She smiled with the pun truly intended. She kissed my forehead and joined Michael and the other girl—Blondie, I'll call her. Michael truly indulged and appeared to float on cloud nine, but as his testosterone levels reached toxic levels and the female pheromones intoxicated us, I saw a side of him I did not recognize. Like a god, he started to dominate the girls. His voice became more authoritative; his movements were more abrupt and forceful. A sense of violence entered the room. His fingers seemed to leave more blanching on the skin. The intensity rose. Lust left; anger entered. I felt uneasy in the voyeur's armchair at the end of the bed. At some point, Michael was behind

Blondie. He stroked her hair away and leaned over to whisper something in her ear. She declined his request with a discreet shake of her head. The answer was clearly 'no,' but she kept smiling and moaning and rolling her hips. It was obvious she did not want to move the action in the direction Michael wanted, but she still wanted to play. She stayed on her elbows as Michael went back to his more upright position. His face hardened; his green eyes turned black, and his brow came down. I could see a darkness consume him. *Who is this?* An uneasy chill made the air tense. Cold. Hard. In a forceful way, he slid his hand all the way down her spine, into the area she had clearly forbidden him just a few moments before. I could see his forearm muscles bulge as his fingertips left deep, white blanches on her skin.

Suddenly she stiffened and arched backwards. Everything froze. Her flowing pelvic actions stopped abruptly. She shot her one hand back and took hold of the wrist on Michael's offending hand. I could hear her whisper, "No, that's not for me honey, but let us get you what you want." Michael's black eyes stared right at her. Every muscle in his body seemed to tense. The tension and silence hung suspended.

Like hearing a loud crack in the ice sheet you were standing on, everyone knew something was going to give way at any second. I sat frozen. *What the hell?*

The girls sensed it as well, and I could see a momentary glance between them. Busty was trying to break the tension. She quickly slipped in close to Michael, warmly kissing him and trying to break the spell. She took his trespassing hand off Blondie and placed it in on her buttocks. It appeared Busty was willing to fulfil Michael's request. However, Michael clearly wanted it his way. He did not change position and was still fully focused on Blondie. The thread of tension was about to snap.

Busty tried to squeeze her way between Michael and Blondie. Strong with alcohol and ego, he violently pushed Busty off the bed and grabbed hold of Blondie's hips with both his hands.

The next moment it was as bright as day in the room. When my eyes adapted, I saw three muscular, 250-pound security guys in tuxedoes pinning Michael down on the bed.

In a raspy voice, the guy without a neck said, "No means *no*, sir. You're done for the night. Let's go!"

Minutes later we were bundled into our limo and sent packing back to Vegas. I was still dazed, but Michael quickly reverted to his old self. "Well, you won't know if you don't go!" he laughed. He popped more champagne and we drank through the night on the Vegas strip.

The rest of our Vegas trip was a blur. I don't know whether it was legal or illegal, paid for or free, but Michael certainly got all his requests fulfilled. I wasn't in the mood for participation, but I did become the freaky voyeur.

As witness to Michael's conquests, I was surprised by its personal fulfilment for me. Enjoyment without participation—the essence of modern entertainment.

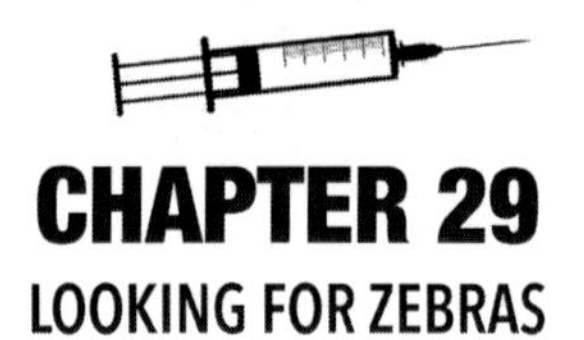

CHAPTER 29

LOOKING FOR ZEBRAS

When Tracy handed me the chart for my next patient in the psychiatry room, I read the brief triage note, which read, "Hearing voices." The community mental health team worker had already seen her and made the recommendation for admission to the mental health unit for a psychotic episode. I quickly read through the initial assessment and specific phrases caught my eye: 'morbidly obese,' 'low mood,' 'very low self esteem,' 'compulsive eater,' 'experimented with drugs to lose weight,' 'speed, cocaine?' 'recent loss of a friend by suicide (jumped off the Peterson Bridge),' 'someone talking to her.' 'Auditory hallucinations/thought intrusion?' 'Recommendation: admission for assessment.'

I walked into the room, still looking down at the chart. I flipped back and saw the printed name: Amelia Blair. I made no connection, but when I saw her face I recognized it immediately. She was the large girl I'd seen New Year's Day. It was her friend who had died recently.

"Hi, Amelia. I'm Doctor Benáde." I drew the chair closer to her bed and sat down. She looked up when I greeted her. Mascara was smeared around her eyes, and thick black streaks ran streams onto her cheeks. Her hair appeared wet and hung over her face. She looked terrible. I could see her trying to figure out where she had seen me before.

"I saw you a couple of months ago. I think you were looking for diet pills then." I was obliged to ask the rhetorical question. "Did they help a bit?" Looking at her, I knew the answer. I guessed she must've picked up at least thirty pounds since I'd seen her last. She knew I was just being courteous. She lifted her elbows outwards and pointed with her hands towards her body. In an outwards motion with her hands, she showed her hips had expanded. She slowly shook her head from side to side, and more tears ran down her cheeks. *Poor girl. It's a struggle.*

We sat in silence for a few moments.

"What happened, Amelia?"

Silence.

"I don't know...."

Silence.

"Okay, let's make it easy. Let's start somewhere." I started with things I could verify to try to distinguish between truth and delusion.

"How did you get here today?"

"I called 911 and they picked me up; then they brought me here."

"Do you know where you are?" She looked at me as if I was the biggest idiot on earth, sighed, and said, "Kamloops Hospital."

"Why did you call 911?"

"I can't really remember—it's all so strange. I felt weak. Dizzy, I guess? All I remember is waking up from the darkness. I was lying on the kitchen floor. I thought I had come back from the dead...." She appeared to be piecing it all together in her mind. "My legs must've just given out. I couldn't move. I just lay there in the kitchen. My arms were so weak, I struggled to lift the phone to dial, and it lay right next to me. I must've dropped it? I couldn't move anything else. My legs felt like they weighed a ton. I could feel them, but I couldn't move them. It's all fuzzy...."

I needed to cautiously tease out the hallucinations. Some patients still have enough insight to know not to admit to them and can shut down in an attempt to hide the delusions. Nobody really wants to be locked up in a mental health unit.

Amelia was likely one of those patients, since she appeared coherent enough. So I tried to find some physical explanation for what had happened to her.

"Did someone attack you? Was there an intruder in your house? You said something to triage about someone talking to you?"

Silence.

"Were you physically assaulted?"

"No?" she ventured. She shook her head as if to rattle it and get the facts into order.

I leaned in and said in a soft tone, "Amelia, you are safe here. Did you hear someone talk to you? Was there someone? It's okay."

"No! ... No?"

Her eyebrows wrinkled in perplexity. She did the quick head-shake again.

"But you heard something, didn't you?"

"I don't really know. It sounded real. Maybe there was someone? I could hear him talk. No, not talk. It was like a whisper. The air became heavier and heavier. I had to focus on just breathing. I felt it all being sucked from me. No power. Weaker and weaker." Her voice started to quiver. Tears ran down her cheeks. She sniffled and grabbed a tissue. "I thought I was dying. I couldn't breathe anymore. I could feel death choking me. I wanted to breathe, but I couldn't. Everything was hazy. I closed my eyes and slowly floated out of my body. I was up at the ceiling looking down at myself, lying there on the kitchen floor. Fat and ugly, dying in front of the refrigerator. The door was open and the fridge light threw a spotlight over my body. I thought, 'How appropriate.' I let go. It felt great just being out of this huge body. I felt light. I was leaving it behind. I floated in the silence, into the darkness. I was so scared, but it was so peaceful. It had to be better than this place. I could hear a whisper echo in the shadows."

"What did the voice say?"

She looked up. "The same stuff I've been saying for years. 'You've got to take control of yourself. You've got to stop eating so much. You've got to lose weight. You are going to die.' Stuff like that. It was like hearing my own thoughts, but in someone else's voice. It was scary. It freaked me out. I wanted to yell at him, 'It's not that fucking easy!' I wanted to scream, but I couldn't move my lips."

"Was it a voice you recognized?"

She stared at the floor in thought, then shook her head slowly and shrugged. "I don't know.... Maybe it was God?"

Silence.

"I think I lost my faith a while ago. I prayed and prayed and prayed, but He never answered before. Maybe this was His voice? Maybe He answered for once? Just like a god to be freaky like that. Maybe it was Death? Aren't they the same thing? Doesn't God bring Death? I thought He had come to get me. I thought for sure that—" Her lower lip quivered and the tears pooled in her eyes. "I was going to die." She burst into tears.

She'd had quite strong delusional thoughts. I wondered whether they were drug induced. She was new to the drug scene; maybe she mixed things up a bit. It was an interesting case; it appeared straightforward, but I always worried about easy answers in life. Maybe there was something else going on. I considered some components of a conversion disorder. Maybe there was even an organic medical explanation.

I felt I needed an opinion from neurology. She had regained all her physical strength, but she'd been convinced she couldn't move. Alternatives started going through my mind: *temporal epilepsy, maybe a tumour.... Maybe a pituitary tumour? It would explain the weight gain. I should check for hirsutism. The tumour could cause a seizure, and then Todd's paralysis thereafter.... an organic explanation. "Look at the clever boy...."* For a moment I loved medicine again. All the little cogs in my brain were spinning. My mind was grabbing all the loose strings and tying them into a beautiful knot of diagnosis. I hoped she didn't have it, of course, but it would be such an interesting diagnosis. I needed to get her medically cleared before psychiatry took over. They'd never look for that.

"Amelia. I need to ask you a few other questions. They might appear a bit strange."

"OK."

"Do you have abnormal hair growth for a woman? Like hair on your navel, or a beard? Hair around your nipple areas? It's called hirsutism."

She looked at me oddly. "Yes."

Check.

"Do you get migraines or headaches?"

"Lots."

Check.

"Do you get dizzy and have balance problems?"

"Yes."

Check. Check. Check. It could be.

"Have you ever had a seizure or convulsions before?"

"Not that I know of."

Maybe not.

I did a complete neurological physical examination and did not find anything significant. I did notice the track marks on her arms that indicated recent drug use, but there weren't the old scars of chronic users. She had a bruise on her shoulder, probably from the fall. She had a bruise on her head, but a fall could have explained that too. She was off-balance when standing and walking, which might support my working diagnosis, but her visual fields examination was normal and all her other examinations were perfect.

I was nonetheless motivated to make a most interesting diagnosis. I got busy. I ordered the brain scan. I called the neurologist in my excitement and gave him the history.

"Sounds very much like psych to me," he said.

"I know it could be psych, but think about it. If she has a pituitary brain tumour with seizures, it could explain her excess growth hormone, obesity, and her loss of consciousness."

"Well, then you'll need to call neurosurgery anyway...."

"Sure, sure. But an alternative diagnosis could be temporal lobe epilepsy. She would have delusions and hallucinations, and seizures with time loss due to that, and then, of course, conversion disorder. Would you mind having a look at her?" Conversion disorder patients got true neurological symptoms due to emotional triggers and could be very difficult to diagnose, because they were one hundred per cent convinced their symptoms were real, even though no one could find physical cause.

He sighed. “Yes, Peter, I will come down later and have a look at her, but first get the brain CT and drug screen done. OK?” He repeated, “You do realize this is probably going to be psych, right? Drug-induced psychosis most probably. Common things occur commonly.”

Tracy called me back to see Amelia. She was getting agitated.

On the CCTV she was pacing up and down the room like a caged tiger. She was clearly worked up, mumbling and talking to herself. Or to someone in the room.

I entered to try and calm her down.

She was mumbling, but slowly she raised her voice. “He drained me. He sucked it from me; I couldn’t even breathe. Why didn’t He take me? What’s the sense in that? Why? Should I do something? Is there a reason?” She was pacing faster and faster. More loudly she said to the ceiling, “Why did you send me back?” Her eyes scanned the room suspiciously. A padded bed was bolted to the floor. A toilet and sink were bolted to the wall. A camera. A solid door. She kept looking at the ceiling in suspicion.

“*What do you want from me?*”

It was so sudden I jumped. Tracy came running in. I slowly backed off towards the door. Keeping an eye on Amelia, I whispered to Tracy behind me, "Call a code white please. I think we will need to settle her down. I'll keep talking to her." I needed to sedate her to get the CT done.

After the yell, she slumped down on the bed.

"I can feel Him. He's here," she mumbled. She shivered, then twitched, and looked abruptly to her right, then down at the floor, then suddenly up at the closed-circuit camera in the corner.

"What did He say?" I probed.

She panicked. "Shhhh, He might hear you. He knows everything, He hears everything, He knew everything."

Then she started mumbling to herself. "I didn't believe her. I should've believed her...."

"Sorry, Amelia, could you repeat that? Believe who?" Maybe her friend's death had triggered the episode? Emotional trauma could trigger a psychotic episode. I ventured a guess in a soft tone.

"Doherty? Are you talking about Doherty?"

As soon as I said it, I knew it was a stupid idea. It flipped her out completely. I could see the paranoia take hold of her in a moment. Her eyes flashed distrust. She jumped up in anger. She was very threatening and stared me in the eyes. "*How do you know? How do you know?*" she screamed.

Ill. Paranoid. Scared. Angry. Dangerous.

There was no more I could do.

I slipped out of the door quickly and punched in the lock code.

I waited for the whole code white team—for aggressive patients—to gather. Amelia kept pacing. When we had our drugs drawn up and the plan talked through, we entered quickly and in force. She was subdued on the bed and given a large dose of a sedative and antipsychotic. We slipped out and waited for it to work. Half an hour later, she was sleeping, and we took her for the brain scan.

Unfortunately, when the neurologist arrived, Amelia was still sleeping and too drowsy to be evaluated properly.

When her brain scan turned out normal, I found myself slightly disappointed because my chance of making an interesting diagnosis appeared unlikely. *It's not about you. This is a young girl's life on the line. Snap out of it.*

Neurology would get her back for an outpatient EEG for epilepsy. After a discussion between the psychiatrist and neurologist, we made a working diagnosis of drug-induced psychosis, or first psychotic episode due to emotional trauma. She would be admitted to the mental health unit if nothing else was found.

She settled down after a few hours, and the drug screen lit up like a Christmas tree. Since there were no beds in the rest of the hospital, she stayed in emergency. The same police officer to bring her in brought in someone else later the same day. I asked him about the circumstances at Amelia's place. He said drugs were everywhere. When they arrived, they found a syringe on the floor close to her left arm and a phone in her right hand. They suspected she was new to the drugs and took too big a hit.

Initially, she was admitted to the medical ward to wait for the drugs to clear her system. All her female hormones, growth hormones, and thyroid hormones were normal. No endocrine abnormalities were found on an extensive workup. Her MRI, to look for a small tumour, was negative. I felt a bit stupid looking for a 'zebra'—medical slang for a rare disease you practically never diagnose—but I knew that if I didn't look, I'd never ever find it. Trying to connect the dots had always been my favourite part of medicine.

After Amelia had been medically cleared, she was transferred to the mental health unit with a diagnosis of drug-induced psychosis and discharged a few days later with a referral for counselling and rehabilitation at addiction services.

After one of my shifts, I quickly snuck over to the mental health unit to check in on her. Outpatient follow-up had already been arranged, as she had specifically asked to see a dietician. She seemed fine. She was convinced God had instructed her to lose weight. "God does not mess around. He has given me another chance. I know now He is not like people think He is. He scared me. He gave me a clear order, and I am sure if I don't fix this, He'll come and get me. Everybody says when you die you go towards the light. They are wrong, Doc. I tell you, it is peaceful, but it is *dark*. It is scary. This is my last shot."

I didn't know what to make of it, especially since I felt empathy for her. Clearly the antipsychotics had settled her emotions, but her delusion was fixed and still very real to her. She seemed optimistic enough, however, and if her delusion made her lose weight, what was the harm? Her unwavering belief in something non-existent struck a chord with me.

I could sympathize with the sickening, helpless conviction that something was real, but without having proof. I felt the same way about Sandra. Something was different with her. She wasn't interested in me. I couldn't see it or prove it, but somehow I just knew it. The more I suspected Sandra of having an affair, the less I found. This only worsened my suspicion. I felt things were being hidden from me. Being told I was paranoid made me suspicious of whoever said it. It was a vicious circle.

I even got the impression that Michael had stopped believing me, but as a friend he continued to listen. He probably thought I was paranoid as well, but he knew me so well that he stopped saying it. The paranoia did not disappear, regardless of how many facts contradicted it.

At that moment all these thoughts were dominating my mind, and when I looked up, most of the nursing staff was looking at me strangely. I found myself standing in the middle of the emergency room again. Another shift, another day. It all blended into one eventually. I must have drifted off.

"What?" I said.

Caroline looked at me knowingly. "You've been standing there looking towards the psych room for so long we thought you were having an absence seizure or something. Are you okay? You seem very distracted." She nudged the back of my upper arm lightly as if to start me working again.

"We're very backed up in here, Peter. Would you mind seeing the lady in cubicle four? She's been here for five hours." Trust Caroline to pull me right back into the chaos.

I walked into the cubicle, looked at the chart, and made an effort. "Hello, I am Dr. Benáde, the emergency doctor. How can I help?"

"Woo, that's interesting. Where are you from?"

It took everything in me to bite my tongue. I wanted to say it was none of her damn business. In fact, I wanted to say I was from Kamloops. She might as well have said, "Hey, you fucking foreigner, what are you doing here?"

My extreme irritation with a harmless question took me by surprise. I had to take a moment to regroup. I blushed and took a deep breath. "You mean my accent? Yes, I am from South Africa."

Some days have a knack of kicking you while you are down and never letting up. I felt ambushed by anger and hostility at every corner. Alarms were everywhere. Babies were crying inconsolably. Nurses were slow. Intravenous pumps kept beeping. The patient buzzers were flashing and making their *ping-pung, ping-pung.* Phones were ringing unanswered while nurses stood next to them. Receptionists seemed to be on breaks or covering 'the other desk' all day. The sounds and noises spiralled to a crescendo of chaotic sound.

I was about to explode, when suddenly Michael did. I saw him take a patient's chart in his hands and smash it on the floor. He absolutely lost it, yelling at gorgeous Tracy. She was quivering. "You need to check the patient's name before you give drugs! Especially for insulin! It's the bloody basics of nursing! Check the name! *Check the fucking name!*" He tapped with his index finger on the chart as he yelled in her face.

"I am so sorry! They switched the patients while I was on break. Mr. Armstrong and Mr. Armitage. I am so sorry. I should have checked." Tracy was in tears. Everyone in the ER was staring at them.

"Get me another nurse that knows what the fucking hell is going on, and *someone* get me fifty CCs of fifty per cent dextrose *now*!" He fixed the patient's problem by giving him glucose, since it appeared that Tracy had accidentally given insulin to the wrong patient. It was a big slip-up, but there was no need to react in such a manner. The patient was clearly fine and made a quick recovery.

I had never heard Michael swear publicly like that. Caroline, too, was clearly upset with Michael's management of the situation and walked over to him for a quick whisper in the ear. She must've asked him to leave, because he walked out and didn't return for the last hour of his shift.

I was still living at his place. When I got there after my shift, I found him sitting downstairs in the darkness by his fireplace. He held a glass of whiskey against his forehead.

"Are you okay, Michael? I've never seen you react like that."

"Tough day."

"No shit."

Silence settled. I poured myself a drink. I loved the sound of the ice cubes smoothly tumbling into the glass, and the crackle as the whiskey split them open.

"Who said that great quote you love so much—what's the guy's name? 'We judge ourselves by what we know we are capable of doing, while others judge us by what we have already done.'"

"Henry Wadsworth Longfellow. Are you making judgements or having regrets?"

He smiled and toasted my glass as he got up to pour himself another. I looked at the glass coffee table in front of me. I saw it, but it didn't register in my mind till months later. It was too late by then. Hindsight is twenty-twenty.

The one corner of the glass table was faintly dusted in white.

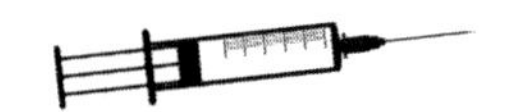

CHAPTER 30

BE CAREFUL WHAT YOU WISH FOR

I was getting ready to do a night shift when something started nagging at me. Something about Sandra. After I moved out, Sandra appeared happier, which I thought was reasonable. However, when I picked up some of my stuff earlier that day, she looked positively cheerful. She had those full lips. I knew the look, but I had not seen it for years.

I had a rhythm and set schedule of little things I did to get me in the right state for the night shift. I would go for a run or cycle in the afternoon, have a good stretch, then have dinner, prepare a sandwich for the night shift, put my phone on the charger, and go to sleep around seven. At ten, I'd get up, shower, and get ready to go. The night shift started at eleven. On the way to work, I would pull in to Tim Horton's to pick up coffee and doughnuts for the nurses. The coffee shop had just run out of coffee as I pulled into the drive-through. The youngster serving me apologized and asked me to pull into a parking spot to wait; they would "quickly brew a fresh batch."

Waiting for the coffee, I checked my phone for messages or emails. And then I saw it. In the top bar on my phone, the small location services arrow blinked on then disappeared. It was there for a fleeting moment. *Which app is using my phone's location?* I quickly scrolled into my phone's settings to check, and next to 'Find My Phone' was the purple arrow. *What?* Obviously I wasn't looking for my phone. *Sandra?* She was the only one with access to my account. But why was she checking on me? Did she need to confirm that I was actually going to work?

All the inconsistencies fell into place. The unexpected cheerfulness, the sparkling eyes, the full lips.... It suddenly made sense. She was expecting a lover while I was at work.

I jumped when the coffee shop attendant knocked on the window with the coffee. I felt frazzled, but drove to work anyway, my brain in overdrive.

At work, I couldn't focus. I needed to get out of there. I needed to confirm my suspicion. *Is Sandra screwing someone while I am examining an old lady with dementia?*

I asked Tracy, *hush-hush*, to lock out a dose of anti-nausea medication for me. When she gave it to me, I whispered, "thanks" and quickly swallowed it with a glass of water. I waited a few minutes for her to take her break. She was stunning to look at, but a gossip. She'd quickly tell the other nurses in the break room that I had a stomach bug. No secrets were safe in the ER. I rushed into washroom, wet my hair a bit, dabbed my forehead with water, and came out a few minutes later.

I approached the other doctor on duty. It was Andy. "Listen buddy, I know you're off shift in two hours, but I just developed this gastro thing. I need to step out for a few minutes until the drugs kick in. Then I'll finish the night shift. Would you cover for me for a bit?"

"Sure, sure," he said, hoping, I was sure, that he wouldn't have to stay for the night.

"I'll get some fresh air."

I slipped out and jumped in my car. I had never done anything like it before, but I needed to know. *She's having an affair. It's the only thing that makes sense.* I promised myself that if this turned out to be a wild goose chase I would lay the paranoia to rest forever. As I neared the house, I turned into a small cul-de-sac and parked the car. I jogged the last 100 metres and softly snuck round the outside of the house towards the back. The back of our house faced the mountain, so we didn't care too much about leaving curtains drawn. My heart raced. I actually felt excited. Anxiety would have been normal, but excitement was strange.

I took a deep breath and peeked through the bedroom window ... and there it was.

Holy shit. I knew it.

As Sandra straddled Michael, her beautiful buttocks were in a slow roll, but started to pick up speed.

With her head tilted backwards, her long hair nearly reached her lower back. Michael had his head popped up on a pillow and appeared to be in a trance. At some point, he lifted his head and his face disappeared between her breasts.

What am I feeling?

This would be most people's worst nightmare, one in which they would storm into the room or hurt someone. They would become angry, rush off, and never return. There I stood with a glorious hard-on experiencing a complete emotional checkmate.

Anger? No. Hatred? No. Relief? Maybe ... victory. I was bloody right!

The reality of it struck me. I was right, but now what?

I watched in fascination as those bodies moved in symphony.

Sandra started to slow down her pelvic rhythm as she anticipated the shudder. Then it came. Like a tsunami wave, it engulfed her whole body and she embraced its force by grabbing onto Michael with all her strength. Her mouth opened soundlessly and every fibre of her muscle seized as it flushed over her body rhythmically. I had never been able to elicit such a response from her. I'd only seen it once, sixteen years before....

My knees buckled as I felt the warm moisture in my pants.

What a release.

As my glance moved from Sandra to Michael, I experienced uncomfortable feelings of betrayal and anger, so I returned my gaze to Sandra's beautiful curves.

As a trophy, I quickly took a video with my phone.

I could breathe again. I felt redeemed for being right, but also conflicted. I found something I didn't know I was looking for, a small last piece of an unsolved puzzle.

Be careful what you wish for—it might come true.

I needed to get back to the hospital, and on the drive back, my mind mulled over everything.

Initially I thought I'd seen Sandra's betrayal, but I quickly realized that I'd witnessed something else: Sandra's choices. Glimpses from the past fell into place. That evening in the beach house so many years ago, when Sandra put her left hand on the doorpost and turned to me, she made a choice. She chose me. Love is a choice.

That is true love, isn't it?

But everything has a price. Now I knew: by choosing me, Sandra sacrificed the sexual fulfilment that Michael offered. I suddenly understood the vision that had bothered me on our legendary night so many years ago. I understood why Sandra never allowed such a night to happen again.

My mind had blinded me from that reality until now.

What if no one person could fulfil your needs? What if you needed to choose between a brief orgasm and a life of companionship?

In reality, we all sometimes doubt our past choices. Milan Kundera said, "*Einmal ist keinmal.* The dress rehearsal for life is life itself." How do we know we have made the right choices in life if we only live once?

Sandra was revisiting her choice.

■ ■ ■

At the hospital, I had to change into my emergency scrubs, but everybody thought I had gastro, so no one made a comment. The night shift passed without incident. I felt completely calm, and nothing could upset me.

Ironically, Michael was the doctor relieving me the next morning. He walked in and greeted me without any indication of guilt for having had sex with my Sandra the previous night. *Did he sleep there?* He showed no signs of his betrayal. He was cool and calm. *Why would you do that? You're supposed to be my friend.* My marriage was in trouble, Grim Reaper was killing my patients, and I felt discontentment with my career; but the one thing I trusted, ever since I had jumped off that bridge, was our friendship. He'd just knocked over the last pillar of my stability.

After the night shift, I sat in the car for a few minutes. Finally, I emailed the video clip to Sandra with a quote from the movie *Magnolia*: "The book says, 'We might be through with the past but the past ain't through with us.'"

My body shook as something broke in me, and

the tears rolled down my cheeks. I was right about my suspicions. Confronting her with it would emphasize the fact that something was missing in our relationship, but I also saw the whole picture of choices made by her. I needed to decide how important Sandra was to me. Nobody was perfect. *My Theia....*

Sandra called. Her tone was warm and relaxed. She seemed relieved that I knew. "I'm sorry, Peter. What else can I say? I just wanted to feel it again. The youth ... the freedom ... the choices we made, you know?"

"I realized what it was about. I could feel it, too. That night.... I miss those times too, but we're not there anymore." I paused for a while. "Where do we go from here?"

A long silence hung in the air.

"I hope the waves are still breaking over those pebbles?" she said.

"As sure as the moon is in the sky."

"Please come home, Peter."

CHAPTER 31

JANE DOE

It was a cool November evening when the ambulance brought in a frail young woman who had been found out by Pat Lake, a little trout lake west of Kamloops. The ambulance crew relayed the story. It was pure luck that she was discovered, since the fishing season had already ended and no ice fishing was allowed on the lake. The person who saw her had been riding the old forestry dirt roads on a mountain bike. All he saw was a piece of coloured clothing sticking out of the yellow grass on the far side of the lake. He almost ignored it, but when he recognized a human foot, he dialled 911. The fire rescue and ambulance took nearly an hour to get around the lake and marsh to get to her. She was on the verge of death.

They transferred her to the bed and she made some moaning, mumbling sounds.

"Is she still a Jane Doe?" Caroline asked.

"Yeah. We couldn't make out a word she said. Her vitals are pretty crappy, Doc," the paramedic added for my benefit. "Blood pressure was low—systolic 90. She looks dry. She has a temp: 38.4. Blood sugar low-ish." He looked at his chart. "It's 3.2. Probably septic, eh, Doc?"

"Sounds suspicious. We'll take it from here. Thank you, boys." They completed the handover but hung around in the trauma room out of curiosity.

I leaned over her and rubbed her breastbone with my knuckles. "Hello! Hello! Can you open your eyes?"

She sort of gazed at me and kept mumbling.

"What's your name?" I rubbed the breastbone hard. "What's your name?"

No response. She kept mumbling, but grabbed my hand and pushed it away from her chest. That was a good sign.

I turned to the medical clerk. "Could you get me the social worker on duty? They can work with the police to figure out who she is. Caroline: Can you or Tracy clean her up a bit and get her dry? She smells, eh? There is grime and dirt underneath her nails. She has a fever, so I wouldn't be too concerned about warming her for exposure."

"What do you think it is?" Tracy asked.

"Delirium. We'll have to work her up to see why. Could be drugs or sepsis, even psychiatric fugue. She's obviously been through some sort of trauma. People get traumatic amnesia for terrible events. They forget who they are and where they're from and end up in unknown places."

I started to examine her. She suddenly appeared familiar.

"Caroline, does she look familiar to you? You know all the frequent flyers. Her face rings a bell somewhere."

"No, I don't know her."

"No fresh intravenous tracks on the arms, but there are some older scars. Maybe she's been through rehab. She's not an obvious junkie."

"It's a weird place for a junkie to show up," Tracy pitched in. "They usually come from an alley downtown, not from way out there in the bush. Something happened to this girl, I tell you. I have a bad feeling about this."

"I agree, but let's focus on the medicine and let the police do the rest."

I continued my examination. Besides the obvious signs of exposure, she had a very swollen left ankle and leg. The injuries looked recent and suggested that she was injured during her ordeal. She was in poor shape. Michael was in emergency and walked over to assist me.

"Let's keep those fluids pumping, Caroline. Hi, Michael. You heard the story. Thanks for helping. She looks pretty unwell. I think it's probably sepsis, but I don't know the cause. Assault? Trauma? Any thoughts?"

He shrugged. "I think you're on the right line. Cover it wide and then work the details and causes. Want me to start some antibiotics?"

"Sure, thanks."

Caroline had already organized two intravenous lines, and the patient was receiving warm fluids intravenously. Caroline commissioned Tracy to quickly clean her up with warm washcloths. I also involved the sexual assault team to review her.

I did my paperwork while they examined her and took her clothes for analysis in case some evidence or history was to emerge later. From the physical examination, the sexual assault physician reported no signs of abuse or rape, but mentioned that her body was battered and bruised all over.

What happened to her? Am I missing something? I re-examined her thoroughly and noticed that the bruise distribution was all over her knuckles (as if she'd hit something with her fists), her knees (as if she'd been crawling on a hard surface), and her shoulders.

Eventually she was clean and in a hospital gown. I was completing my secondary abdominal examination when something that I hadn't noticed on my initial exam struck me.

Holy shit. "Caroline. Look at all this loose skin and this skin apron over her pubic area. She recently lost a ton of weight."

I looked up at her face, and finally, I recognized her.

"Amelia! It's Amelia!"

When I mentioned the name, there was a glimpse of recognition in her eyes. It *was* Amelia Blair. *What the hell had happened to her?*

I contacted the police investigator, told him that I knew the victim, and gave him her details. The investigator phoned me back about thirty minutes later. Amelia's mother had filed a missing persons report about two months prior.

Amelia had an undisplaced fracture of her ankle and two broken bones in her hands. The fractures in her hands—of the fifth metacarpals—were typical boxing fractures. After the intensive fluid therapy, she appeared more stable.

My shoulders dropped when I saw who was on call for ICU: Halstead. As always, the ICU was very full, so Halstead was grilling me over the phone for the reasons she required ICU. I had to admit, she was relatively stable, and she wasn't intubated or on any life support. Her vital signs were improving, and although she was ill, she was probably a little too healthy for the ICU at that point. She would have to go to one of the wards.

I gave the okay. Michael mixed a last bag of antibiotics and placed it at her feet. The infusion would be continued upstairs, so Amelia was wheeled out of the department.

CHAPTER 32

DAY 69

Thirteen stacks and four lines.

She started to slowly undress, because everything needed to be done slowly now. She was so weak. She folded her clothes on the bed because it looked neat and was something to do. Naked, she walked to the sliver of light that crossed the room. In its light, she examined her body. It was interesting to see how it had changed. She never used to look at herself. There was too much shame and guilt in the mirror. She looked so different now. The skin flaps looked funny and thin as they hung down like shower curtains from her breasts, stomach, and arms. Her hands looked so strange with the sticklike fingers she now had. Gone were the sausage fingers. Her 'kankles'—the derogatory name for her fat ankles that looked like knees—were gone too. A thin skin layer draped her anklebones like a pulled-down sock. She wore her skin like a boy wore a man's suit.

I am so close. Don't get too excited. Life had always disappointed her; why would it be any different this time? *Limit your expectations to avoid disappointment....*

"Strip," the voice said.

She smiled, as she was nude already. The light came on, and she felt her heart pound in her chest as she stepped forward. She looked down at the spinning dial.

It had been months since the voice said, "Here's the key to your freedom. Reach your ideal weight of 140 pounds and I will set you free. To be thin: you asked and you shall receive."

I never thought I'd ever get close to that magical number, and now it's so close. Can I trust him to stick to his word?

The scale dialled rolled and started to slow down at 137, 138, 139.... *Stop. Stop. Stop. Could it be?*

It stopped.

140.

"Yeah!" she yelled.

Goosebumps rose on her arms as her heart jumped from her chest. Then she cringed and closed her eyes.

"Please, please, please no buzzer," she murmured.

There was silence for what felt like an eternity.

"You asked and you have now received," the voice said. "Congratulations. You have been petrified thin." Like the recording on an old tape recorder, the voice kept repeating in its slow distorted tone: "Petrified thin." A loud tape rewinding sound played. "Petrified thin." The tape rewinding sound again. "Petrified thin." The repetition slowed down and finally the voice's tone became so extremely deep it sounded like a harbour foghorn dramatically echoing out the final word: P-E-T-R-I-F-I-E-D"

Silence.

A loud mechanical noise could be heard on the roof as a motor kicked into action. The blinding white daylight hit her naked body as the big door swung open automatically. She shielded her eyes from the light, grabbed her clothes, and ran.

Run, run, run for your life, her brain screamed at her. She fell three or four times in the first twenty yards. She was way too weak to run, but she did it anyway. When she could see the box no longer, she stopped and quickly pulled on some clothes.

She struggled to see in the overwhelming daylight. The next moment, she felt weightless as she stumbled over a cliff. She hit the ground pretty hard but scrambled back up and kept going through the brush. She was exhausted. She kept falling, but she ran until she couldn't any more. She fell down one last time and crawled till it all became black.

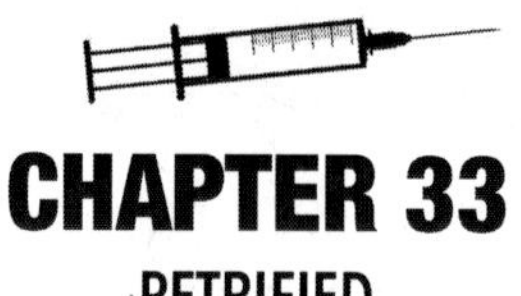

CHAPTER 33

PETRIFIED

"It was an assault ... more an abduction. It was horrific," the police officer blurted. He brought us more information from the scene. "From where we found her, the dogs followed her scent for miles into the mountains. Her trail showed a ten-foot fall down a cliff when she was making her escape. On an extremely desolate spot, high up in the greenstone area, we found an old steel storage container. You know, those big ones you see on the trains. She was locked up in there for sixty-nine days. She marked each day with a scratch on the wall like prisoners do. It's a bit unclear whether she had managed to escape or whether she had been released by her captors, but there was a mechanical contraption on the door lock connected to a cell phone, so we suspect that she was actually released by a phone call. Forensics is still investigating the scene. Anyway, the door was open when we got there. There was a ton of empty plastic water bottles heaped up in the corner, but only traces of food. There was a hatch in the roof where they would drop stuff in to her and remove the sh— um, excrement. In one corner was a small yoga mattress."

"Sounds terrible."

"It's crazy. But the weirdest part of it? In one of the corners there was a bathroom scale, a roof-mounted spotlight, and a small video camera. It was some fucked up weirdo doing this. The camera appeared to be hooked up to the cell phone. Maybe linked to the Internet? There was a small speaker as well. The asshole was able to monitor her with the camera and talk to her. It was clear the camera pointed at the scale ... weird. The container walls were smeared with her blood. She must've been hitting it with her fists and knees all the time. She even dented the side in one spot."

"Sounds like someone was getting off on watching her starve."

"That is some serious S&M shit," the police officer said. "She must've been so scared."

"Petrified," I mumbled.

Tracy spun around. "What did you say?"

She had just returned after taking Amelia to the ward.

"Are you talking to me?" I asked Tracy.

"Yeah. Did you just say, 'petrified'?"

"Yes. I was just talking to Mike here about what that poor girl had been through."

"But you said 'petrified.' That's a freaky coincidence."

"Tracy, what's this about?" She was getting on my nerves.

"'Petrified' is the word she kept mumbling. She freaked me out. She kept saying, 'Petrified thin, petrified thin, petrified thin.' And then she would shiver and whimper."

I could feel the hair on the back of my neck rise, and its muscles seized up. A chill ran down my spine.

No. It couldn't be. Too much coincidence.

I scanned the room looking for Michael.

Petrified. It's his favourite word. *Think, Peter.*

Petrified, scared. Turned to stone, unable to move. Frozen, paralysed with fear.... Paralysed. The penny dropped.

"Where is Michael?" I yelled at Caroline.

"He said he was slipping out for a moment...," she pointed to the roof.

I ran towards the elevators. He had been very strange lately, and I had been getting uneasy chills whenever he expressed his anger towards obese people. And that evening in Vegas, he'd scared me. His eyes were dark; he'd appeared evil. Could he be this evil?

Like a computer going into overdrive, my brain ran through the logic, whatever logic there was to be found. Before, when Amelia had claimed she was assaulted, everyone thought she was psychotic. She was so convincing. She said she couldn't move; that she'd felt paralysed. Of course she did, because he paralysed her! It had to have been him. Nothing else made sense.

Only one guy I knew was clever enough to know this. Only one guy was crazy enough to do it. Only one guy loved the word 'petrified' that much.

I heard the announcement: "Code blue seven north. Code blue seven north."

Shit, shit, shit. He was trying to cover his ass. He was going to kill her. I ran up the stairs, since my legs were quicker than the elevator. I had to out-think him.

If I wanted to paralyse someone, I would use a long-acting paralysing drug. It would stop them breathing, and nobody would be looking for it. *You're clever, Michael, but this time I got you.*

I ran into the ward on the seventh floor. It was a typical code blue scene, with people everywhere. And, as expected, it was Amelia.

"She just stopped breathing" was the report. "Maybe a PE?"

"How long has she been out for?"

"Don't really know. We just had her settled in and she was dozing off to sleep. She wasn't even connected to the monitor yet. The nurse who was going to check her in was on break, and when another nurse walked by, she noticed the patient was blue! She ran in and called the code. It must've been less than five minutes, I guess. It was close, she still had a pulse, but she wasn't breathing."

They were bagging her with a mask and Ambu bag. She needed to be intubated. I walked around the bed, took over, and intubated her. As I looked up, the culprit hung right there in plain sight, with Michael's signature all over it: the bag of 'antibiotics.' I stopped the infusion immediately, grabbed the bag, and ordered a nurse to get me neostigmine right away. She looked at me as if I was from Mars. "Just do it. It's a bloody order. There's been a med error. She's been given a muscle paralyzer. We need to reverse it right now."

I intubated her, and then we transferred her to the ICU, where she would be ventilated till the drugs were reversed. I quickly handed her over to Halstead and conveyed my suspicion that it was caused by muscle paralyzers, but asked him to do the rest of the work-up in case it was something else. He asked how it could have happened, and I just shrugged and shook my head. "I'll find out."

I took the bag that Michael had mixed and ran up to the roof.

CHAPTER 34

BATMAN AND JOKER

As I shouldered open the exit door to the roof, I grimaced at the thought of how many times Amelia must have slammed into the walls of the box to be so bruised. How scared she must have been. *Petrified.*

He was waiting on the roof. Waiting for me. Standing by the edge on the far side of the railing, he slowly dragged in the cigarette smoke. Like in a fairy tale, the first snowflakes of winter swirled down slowly.

I walked towards him with the intravenous bag in my hand. He looked at it and then tilted his head back to catch a snowflake in his mouth.

"Isn't it magnificent how the snow paints everything so beautifully white, covering all the grime as if it never existed?"

"Oh, the shit's still there, no matter how much snow you cover it with." I snapped back.

Michael looked at me.

"What the fuck, Michael? Why would you do it? You locked that poor girl in a box. 'Petrified thin,' she said.... You've always loved that word play. *Are you fucking crazy?*" I yelled. "Jesus, Michael! You wanted to scare her thin? Why? Just to prove your argument? Well done, Michael," I said sarcastically. "You just proved people get thin *when you starve them.* You crossed the fucking line, man."

He still said nothing. He seemed to ignore my rant completely and stared into space. I took a breath of cool air and walked closer. "So it's pancuronium in the bag, isn't it? That's what I would use."

He quickly glanced in my direction. *Gotcha.*

He slow clapped his hands, his cigarette hanging from the corner of his mouth. "Congratulations, Peter," he said as he took the cigarette into his right hand and shot it over the roof edge. One eye was still pinched closed from the cigarette smoke. He held an arrogant stance of defiance.

"You could have killed her in the crate. Why didn't you?"

Silence.

"You arrogant bastard! You wanted to kill her *right here* under my nose and laugh at us all, because you're so fucking smart. You bloody show-off. Well, you screwed up. I got you."

He smiled a cynical smile as he lit another cigarette. But he kept looking for something in my eyes. Was there something I had overlooked? There had to be.... He was waiting for me to connect the dots. *What was it?*

A chill went through my spine. "Bloody hell! She wasn't the only one?"

"Ah. Clever boy gets it."

"*Fuck you.* Who else...? Are you my grim reaper?"

"No, not really ... well, a little bit." He gave a weird chuckle. He appeared calm, as if he had seen this happen in his mind a thousand times over. He simply turned to me and started talking as if it was one of our run-of-the-mill conversations. "Don't make it so personal. I only helped out the ones who needed to go. Some of them were your patients, but it was never aimed against you. Many were thankful. The fractured hip lady, Mrs. Campbell, she was so thankful. She wanted to go, and I let her. That grumpy bastard Patterson was just a grouch and a burden on society; he needed to go. Same with the asshole, steroid-filled drug dealer, Chad Bishop ... and David Morin was an oxygen thief who fucking killed his four-year-old niece, so he had it coming. I could go on." He shot another cigarette butt over the edge.

"You killed them all? And you're telling me this as if it's not bloody crazy." I stepped back, trying to get a grip on it all. "What the fuck? How and why?"

"Oh the why, the why. It simply needed to be done. Someone had to step up and fix the problem. Someone needs to rid society of the fat, the old, the evil, the sponges and burdens. You know I like a challenge, and it has amused me getting it done.

"The how was so easy. You were spot on, Peter. Pancuronium—long-acting muscle paralyser. You're holding my secret potion in your hand, freely available to most physicians. A little dose in the arm or in the intravenous line, and within a few minutes they stop breathing. Timing is everything."

He was right. When someone died unexpectedly, there might be an investigation, but these drugs were rarely traceable. So the coroner would presume a heart attack, stroke, or pulmonary embolism. If it happened to an old lady or a street bum, who was going to ask questions anyway? No one would suspect foul play. *People only see what they expect to see.*

"But why Amelia?"

"Amelia and Doherty ... my little pet projects. People can achieve so much more in life if they are truly motivated.

"Amelia and Doherty had the same weakness as my mom, with no willpower or self-control. Asking to be different but too weak to change. So I gave them the opportunity of a lifetime. I brought the only true motivator in human nature: fear. True fear. The fear only death can instil.

"I paid both of them a visit at their homes just to see if giving them a bit of fearful motivation could get them to achieve what they wanted. I gave them a small dose of suxamethonium. A short-acting paralyzer that reverses on its own. They'd stop breathing whilst fully awake. Just when they thought they were going to die, I told them that they needed to lose weight—or they would actually die. The drug would reverse and they'd wake up again. Scared shitless. I thought that would motivate them, but Doherty jumped off the bridge. However, can you believe Amelia still did not lose any weight? So I thought it was time to truly help her reach her ideal weight. Being religious, she probably asked her god thousands of times to make her thin. Ask and you shall receive, the Bible says. Finally, God gave her what she asked for." He pointed to himself.

"When did you become this monster, Michael?" I mumbled.

"Don't be so melodramatic, Peter. She got what she asked for. And I *did* release her."

"Only to try and kill her tonight."

He shrugged. "I need to look after number one as well," he said with a smile, throwing both his thumbs towards his chest. "And frankly, every day needs a new challenge." I could tell he had been burning with the desire to tell me these things. These confessions clearly unburdened him.

Stunned, I asked, "Anyone else?"

"Well, there is my mom...."

Jesus!

"She was the first one. Sounds bad to do that to your mom, but she was very evil. She was exactly like the Penguin to me. I couldn't stand her anymore. The smell, the stuff she made me do.... She needed to go. I told her it was a flu shot when I jabbed her in the arm with the paralyser. She sat on her couch and I kissed her goodnight on the cheek. No more Mickey this or Mickey that. I walked out the door and waited for the phone call. Her obesity and abuse repulsed me, but worst of all was her weakness." He stared into the distance.

"Son, *do* what needs to be done." He quoted his dad again and smiled.

With his hands on the railing behind him, he hung over the ledge, like a mermaid on the bow of an old pirate ship. The wind gusted against the building and threw his hair back from his face.

He closed his eyes.

I walked to the railing. "Why did you have sex with Sandra? Was that also one of your new challenges? Taking it all to the edge? Running the risk of ruining our friendship? I sort of understand why Sandra did it. But why would you betray me like that?"

"Not actually one hundred per cent clear on it myself. It was just one of those fun things to do." He was being cocky and weirdly calm, like he was high. "And frankly, Catz was the greatest fuck I ever had."

"*Michael.*" I flinched with the hurt he had just inflicted. We held each other's stares. Michael cast his eyes down and bowed his head as a gestured apology.

Silence.

Gusts of icy chill tugged on our clothes and hair. Michael stared out over the city as if it were his. He started talking in a calm and settled tone, nearly contemplative. Serious. "It's not about the 'how' or the 'why.' It's about the 'who.' Who is going to do what needs to be done? This world is going under. The city is falling. Mother Nature has lost. Humanity has risen to be an evil, destructive force. We, with our social structures and modern medicine, have conquered the forces of natural selection. Survival of the fittest is no more. Even the weak, the fat, the crippled, the sick, the evil survive. We keep them alive. We created this world and filled it to overcapacity. We created this evil. Earth is crying for help. The balance needs to be restored. Someone needs to do what needs to be done. You know this, Peter. It is up to me. It's up to us." He looked into my eyes and nearly pleaded. "The people won't see it that way. They don't see the evil, because they are the evil. *We* need to restore the balance; we need to get rid of the evil."

I finally understood Michael's perspective: he was Batman, the saviour with a calling to get rid of evil. He inherited his sense of duty from his dad. And now he wanted me to join him. He wanted Robin's assistance. He knew I'd understand when no one else would.

I put down the IV bag, took a deep breath, and leaned onto the railing next to Michael. Our shoulders touched. A calm sense of understanding hung in the air. I savoured the moment. He looked to me, seeking my reply.

Who has the courage to do what needs to be done? Who will answer the call?

"I know exactly what you mean, Michael."

Michael turned his head towards me. His green eyes pierced my soul. He smiled.

He let go of the railing with his right hand and swung around to hug me.

“I need to let you go.” I gently released his left hand’s grip from the railing.

He needed to fly.

You can’t see evil if you’ve become it.

Batman turned into Joker.

He always took everything in life as it was handed to him, but this time, when I let him go, I noticed a glimpse of surprise. Maybe he didn’t expect I had it in me? The surprise lasted for a fraction of a second, and then he almost appeared proud of me. He embraced what I had handed him: Death.

How cool and fitting were those famous last words, “Why so serious?” And the Joker’s smile. Only my unique friend Michael would do that.

Michael’s death was a momentary victory over Grim Reaper. A villain lay slain in snow, but there was a death in the family. Robin’s heart was broken as well.

CHAPTER 35
THE CAVE

In the aftermath of the incident, an investigation was launched. The focus was on what had happened on the roof. I explained how I'd confronted Michael with his murderous actions and how he confessed to many more. The police presumed he jumped to avoid facing the consequences. I didn't sway their assumptions. The investigation revealed the presence of a long-acting paralyzer, pancuronium, in the intravenous bag. I received some collegial recognition for making the diagnosis so early.

Halstead, of all people, came over to the ER to congratulate me on picking up such a rare presentation. "When you said pancuronium poisoning, I thought you had lost it. And as it turned out, you were bloody right! Well done, Peter. That was brilliant. You saved her." He slapped me on the back as he walked off. "Clever boy."

....with the badge, polishing his trophy. I smiled at the irony: a lifetime of seeking appreciation followed

by my realization of its pointlessness when it finally arrived.

Michael had cocaine in his system, which explained enough for the police.

I felt guilty that I hadn't taken responsibility for the small fact that I'd helped Michael on his merry way down. I knew I'd done the right thing, but remorse still haunted me. Anyway, I had other responsibilities in life. I knew Michael would prefer me to look after those rather than sitting in a cell on his behalf.

The police investigation led to Michael's house, and they found a secret room nestled beneath his bedroom, behind the bar wall in his basement. On the wall was a framed copy of the 1988 *Batman: A Death in the Family* comic book. Its black cover featured Batman hunched over on his knees with the broken body of Robin in his arms. In this edition, Batman and Robin's friendship had broken down, and Robin had died. Batman was filled with grief and remorse.

It was a trophy room. Each villain had a picture and a portfolio of crimes written up for judgment.

His mother, Dorothy, and Amelia were all listed under *the Penguin.*

Chad Bishop—the drug seeker and steroid injector, was *Bane*, maybe because of his big muscles and the 'poison' in his veins.

Earl Patterson was *the Scrooge.* Michael created his own villains, it seemed.

David Morin was *Lock-Up*, his nickname from the time he spent in jail. Michael had displayed newspaper clippings that reported the death of his niece and his conviction for the sexual assault of another eleven-year-old, together with the one-line announcement of his death in the local paper.

In the featured corner of the room, a spotlight highlighted a large, beautifully framed photograph of us: Batman, Robin, and Catwoman at the Halloween party in 1994. We were beautiful and young, the world our oyster.

CHAPTER 36

SEE-SAW

I walked Esmé to the park the Saturday after the investigation concluded. I made an effort to take a stroll with her once a week, just to catch up. Although she was sixteen, she would still walk with me to the park.

"I miss Uncle Michael," she said.

"Me, too darling. A lot."

"Mom misses him too. Her eyes are red every day."

"We were all very close, Esmé. Family, actually."

"You and Mom seem to be fighting less. Are things okay with you guys?"

"You know, we went through a rough patch, but we're doing okay, I think. You need to know yourself before you can work on a relationship. I got a bit lost. Mom did too. We're sorting it out, though. How was your week? Are you okay?"

Before she could answer, she saw the see-saw, and her eyes lit up as if it were the first time ever. She ran towards it and yelled, "I love doing this!"

Still some kid left in her. She got onto the see-saw and balanced herself, standing on one end. With her arms stretched out wide, she slowly walked uphill on the beam towards the fulcrum. Just as she reached the centre, the lower end lifted. There she stood, with one foot on each side of the fulcrum, swaying her weight, balancing the see-saw beam under her feet.

In the see-saw of life opposites meet at a fulcrum....

Good-Evil.

Friend-Foe.

Do we even know when we're at the tipping point?

I was drifting away in thought and didn't notice that I was crying. Esmé noticed, though. She jumped off the see-saw and ran towards me. Taking my face in her hands, she kissed the tears on my cheeks.

"It's gonna be okay, Dad. You should let us in.... Don't you always say, 'Everything has a crack in it; that's how the light gets in'?"

"That was Leonard Cohen."

She put her arms around me, and my shoulders shook as I let it all go. I cried like I had on the hospital roof.

"I love you, Dad."

When I regained my composure, I looked into the emerald green eyes that were her namesake.

"Esmé—Esmeralda. I love you, too."

We hugged for a long time.

Esmé was another consequence of that ecstatic night long, long ago. She was a commitment I would never regret, but one, we knew, Michael would never have made.

Although our friendship had been bound in blood and petrified through time, we cautiously left the Esmé issue to the unsaid moments we shared.

Everything has a crack in it.

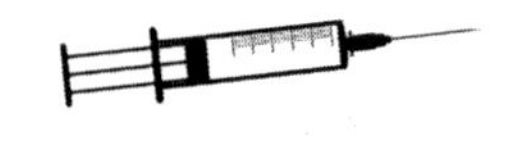

CHAPTER 37

EPILOGUE

December 8, 2011: Jerry Robinson, comic book legend and creator of the Joker, died two weeks after Michael did, at age eighty-nine.

January 30, 2012: I was reading *Time* magazine when an article caught my eye. Written by Alice Park, the title read: "Bat Signal. Bats are dying in record numbers, heralding a real problem for people." It was reported that in the United States, between 5.7 and 16 million bats were estimated to have died since 2006. The bats were all found with white fuzz in their noses, probably caused by a fungus, suffering from what was called white-nose syndrome. The concern was that since bats consumed their body weight in insects every night, the insect population would explode in the future, become a swarming plague, and spread disease.

I smiled. *Life is a see-saw, isn't it*?

I recalled the words Michael used the first time he talked about Batman. "You know what I love most about the whole philosophy behind Batman? Everything is connected. There is no good without evil. There is no light without darkness. Your killer could be the one who makes you laugh. Your saviour might be a masked man dressed in black. The good and the evil exist in both the hero and the villain. The good can create evil, but from the evil, good can be born as well. It's all about the balance." Then a whisper. "New villains will always re-emerge. Balance needs to be restored. The bat will need to rise again."

Who will answer the call?

ABOUT THE AUTHOR

On our journey of uncertainty through life, our biggest challenges quite often blindside us on some idle weekday. During those times, we often seek answers from our peers, friends, elders, teachers, religion and the written word. We share these crossroads with others to enlighten our own perspectives. As a qualified emergency physician, I am privileged to observe the world from a different side. Daily I witness people having the worst and, on occasion, the best days of their lives. I hope to illuminate these crucial, and sometimes dark, moments of life, in a search for clarity and truth. I believe that if you learn to experience life not only through your own senses, but also through the perceptions of your fellow voyagers, your view of life will be completely transformed.

I was born in South Africa and became an emergency physician during the violent era of my birth land's transformation from the ashes of apartheid to a new rainbow nation. In the South African trauma rooms, I witnessed the extreme ability that humans have to inflict misery and pain upon each other and hoped to expose a bit of that brutal world in See-saw.

Currently I am a proud Canadian living in beautiful British Columbia with my wife and our two lovely daughters. "The only certainty in life is uncertainty and thus: Accept what is."

ACKNOWLEDGEMENTS

See-Saw would not have seen the light of day if it wasn't for the feedback, support, and encouragement I received from my friends Alan and Tamara Vukusic, Diana Hauser, and Melinda Uys.

Amanda Bidnall - your editing and feedback was exceptional! Thank you so much.

Crystal Stranaghan - you are "Captain O my Captain" of this ship. You made this happen! I cannot thank you enough for everything you and your team (Constance Mears, Greg Brown, Jared Hunt and Nicole Obre) have orchestrated. You are simply magnificent.

I thank my family for allowing me to escape into my secret world of writing for hours and days on end.

I want to take this moment to thank the staff in emergency rooms all over the world for the tremendous work you do night and day; saving the lives of others. Many of the battles you fight go unseen. Many of the sacrifices you make go unnoticed. In the ER, the abuse staff has to tolerate is astounding and the lack of appreciation unfathomable. I see, I saw, and I thank you.

DISCLAIMER AND REFERENCES

This novel and its characters are fictional. Any resemblance to actual individuals is purely coincidental. In the novel, I have made references to famous fictional characters well known in the public domain, due to the general public's fascination for these figures. The characters in this story quote many famous individuals and these quotes are referenced below.

Pg. 3: Joseph Campbell: "If you are falling ... dive."

Pg. 14: *Batman* – 1989 by Warner Bros Pictures.

Pg. 14: Batman comic – copyrights held by DC Comics.

Pg. 18: From the movie *Revolver* by Samuel Goldwyn Films: "We're approval junkies. We're all in it for the slap on the back and the gold watch. The hip-hip-hoo-fuckin'-rah. Look at the clever boy with the badge, polishing his trophy."

Pg. 21: Mahatma Gandhi: "I am prepared to die, but thoro io no oauco for which I am prepared to kill."

Pg. 25: From the movie *Dead Poet's Society* by Touchstone pictures: "Carpe Diem. Suck the marrow of life."

Pg. 54: *Batman Returns* by Warner Bros. Pictures.

Pg. 63: Edith Piaf: "Non, je ne regrette rien."

Pg. 69: Commonly used motivational quote of unknown origin: "You don't always get what you work for, but you always work for what you get."

Pg. 82: Mae West: "Anything worth doing is worth doing slowly."

Pg. 82: Mae West: "I never said it would be easy, I only said it would be worth it."

Pg. 92: The movie *Batman and Robin* by Warner Bros. Pictures.

Pg. 100: The movie *Batman Begins* by Warner Bros. Pictures.

Pg.101: Detective Comics #67, 1942 *First Penguin Cover in Pen and Ink*, copyright DC Comics.

Pg.101: 1943 Detective Comic #76—*Slay 'em with Flowers*, copyright DC Comics.

Pg. 103: JC Watts: "It doesn't take a lot of strength to hang on; it takes a lot of strength to let go."

Pg. 104: Humphrey Bogart: "Things are never so bad that they can't be made worse."

Pg. 105: From the movie *Casablanca* by Warner Bros. Pictures: "Of all the gin joints, in all the towns, in all the world."

Pg. 109: From the movie *The Dark Knight* by Warner Bros. Pictures: "Why so serious?" and "Let's put a smile on that face."

Pg. 110: Mae West: "Sex is like bridge: If you don't have a good partner you'd better have a good hand."

Pg. 131: Joseph Cossman: "The best bridge between despair and hope is a good night's sleep."

Pg. 132: Mae West: "I never said it would be easy, I only said it would be worth it."

Pg. 143: Mario Andretti: "If everything still feels under control, you're just not going fast enough."

Pg. 144: The song "Sandstorm" was produced by DJ Darude.

Pg. 160: From the musical group Pink Floyd, the song titled "Comfortably Numb."

Pg. 169: From the movie *The Matrix* by Warner Bros. comes the quote, "There is no spoon."

Pg. 198: From Milan Kundera in the book *The unbearable lightness of being*: "Einmal ist keinmal. The dress rehearsal for life is life itself."

Pg. 198: From the movie 1999 *Magnolia* by New Line Cinema: "The book says, 'We might be through with the past but the past ain't through with us.'"

Pg. 222: The 1988 "A Death in the Family" #426 Batman comic copyrights to DC Comics.

Pg. 225: Leonard Cohen from the song "Anthem": "Everything has a crack in it; that's how the light gets in." May the legend rest in peace: we will miss you! - 07 November 2016.

Pg. 227: *Time* magazine, January 30, 2012, by the author Alice Park: "Bat Signal. Bats are dying in record numbers, heralding a real problem for people."